D0094592

RELUCTANT DESIRE

Laura was furious. It was bad enough having to share her home with a stranger for a month — but being forced to live under the same roof as the notorious Adam Veryan ... His midnight-dark eyes challenged Laura to forget about her fiancé Rodney, and she knew instinctively that Adam would be a dangerous, disruptive presence in her life. She'd be a fool to surrender her heart to such careless custody ... but could she resist Adam's flirtatious charm?

KAY GREGORY

RELUCTANT DESIRE

Complete and Unabridged

LINFORD
Leicester

First published in Great Britain in 1995

First Linford Edition
published 2007

British Library CIP Data

Gregory, Kay
   Reluctant desire.—Large print ed.—
Linford romance library
1. Love stories
2. Large type books
I. Title
823.9'14 [F]

ISBN 978–1–84617–756–9

Published by
F. A. Thorpe (Publishing)
Anstey, Leicestershire

Set by Words & Graphics Ltd.
Anstey, Leicestershire
Printed and bound in Great Britain by
T. J. International Ltd., Padstow, Cornwall

This book is printed on acid-free paper

1

The smell of disintegrating halibut penetrated Laura's consciousness at about the same time as she flipped to the page in her history textbook headed *Causes of the Decline and Fall of Ancient Rome*.

'Oh, no,' she groaned, tipping a disgruntled silver-gray cat off her lap and hurrying to the top of the stairs. 'Not the decline and fall of fresh halibut as well. Please, not tonight, of all nights, when I told Rodney I was fixing his favorite fish.' As she hurtled downstairs she wondered despairingly if it was possible to disguise tinned tuna as halibut and came to the conclusion that it wasn't.

She reached the kitchen at full tilt, noticing too late the tan and white rug in the doorway. When she crashed to the floor, the rug, which looked like a beagle but wasn't, came suddenly and indignantly to life.

'Ouch!' said Laura. 'Pal, for heaven's sake, must you always get in the way?'

The rug gave a short, protesting grunt and subsided back on to the floor.

'Move.' She gave it a half-hearted shove, and it shifted a reluctant inch to the right.

With a sigh Laura started to push herself upright, but she had only made it on to her knees when it came to her that something besides the fish wasn't right. Her heart gave an uncomfortable lurch, and she counted to ten, closed her eyes, and then opened them again with great caution.

No, she wasn't hallucinating. Two battered brown sandals were planted on the red kitchen tiles just in front of her. They were occupied by large, masculine feet in heavy black socks. A hand, which presumably came with the feet, was reaching down to help her stand up. She took it and raised her head slowly.

Bending over her was a long,

muscular body dressed in a clean but faded gray turtleneck and well-washed, hip-clinging jeans. The face that went with the body was tanned and healthy-looking. Unusually dark eyes gleamed at her from under upswept black eyebrows that matched dark, almost shoulder-length hair. As Laura swallowed convulsively, she also took in high cheekbones, a slightly crooked nose above a mouth with seductively full lips, and very white teeth that looked as though they ought to be clamped down on a cutlass.

The total effect was raffish, piratical and dangerous. Laura was immediately reminded of one of the more dis-reputable villains from the adventure yarns she had loved so much as a child. But this villain was unexpectedly attractive, and she was surprised by the sudden shiver that traveled down her spine when his hand tightened on hers to swing her easily on to her feet.

'Who are you?' she gulped, her eyes on a level with the slight cleft in his chin. 'What are you doing in my kitchen?'

' 'Thank you' would do nicely,' replied the stranger.

'I beg . . . Oh. All right, thank you. Now what are you doing in my kitchen?' She tried to regain custody of her hand, but he wouldn't release it.

'Rescuing you from the clutches of that animated doorstop.' The reply was laid-back, delivered in a deep, smoky drawl.

Laura, who wanted very much to glare at this pirate king and tell him to get out of her house, remembered in time that she was home alone, and that for all she knew her muscular and uninvited visitor was an escapee from the local detention center.

She dropped her eyes and glared at the animated doorstop instead. Pal heaved a lengthy sigh and thumped his tail on the floor.

When she looked up again she saw that the interloper had stepped back and was surveying her minutely from head to toe. It was an appreciative

4

survey, she noted, suspecting that her cheeks were turning as flame-red as her hair. It occurred to her, briefly, that Rodney had never once looked at her with that expression of irreverent admiration in his eyes. He always said she was too slim and willowy, and ought to put some flesh on her bones. He also said it was a pity that her long, thick hair was so unruly, and insisted she tie it back or put it up.

'I'm glad you leave it loose, blue-eyes,' said the stranger, startlingly echoing her thoughts. He released her hand and tilted her chin toward the summer sun beaming through a white-framed bow window. 'You have an interesting face,' he murmured, as though he had every right to comment. 'Sort of sweet and old-fashioned with that small round chin, and those childish freckles on your nose . . . ' He paused. 'You ought to be wearing lace and ruffles, not that blue check shirt and — no. On second thoughts, 1 have to approve the jeans. They do have a certain appeal.' When she flung round so that her back was to him, he added lightly, 'Especially from that angle.'

Laura gasped, and for a moment expected to feel his large hand coolly exploring that angle, but instead he tapped her on the shoulder. When she turned back to face him, frowning, he gave her a white, tip-tilted grin, and said, 'Don't look so affronted, blue-eyes. It was a compliment.'

'My name is Laura,' she replied. 'And I'd be obliged if you'd keep your compliments to yourself.' He was still grinning, in an admiringly predatory way, and she finished hastily, 'My fiancé and my father will be here any minute now, so — '

'I know.' He nodded with no sign of discomfiture. 'Your father told me about you. That you were born here on Vancouver Island, that you've been keeping house for him in Cinnamon Bay for years, and that you practically brought up your young brother. Ethan, isn't it? He also told me you work in the

6

local bakery. And that somewhere in there you're managing to fit in a college correspondence course in history.' The stranger narrowed his eyes and added softly, 'He also mentioned a sober and upstanding accountant with the improbable name of Rodney Fosdyke. You can't possibly marry him, you know.'

Laura, who had been gazing at him with her mouth open, closed it with a nearly audible snap. But when it came to forming a smart reply to this utterly outrageous assertion she found that, after all, she wasn't up to it. Swift repartee had never been her strong point.

'I-I don't know what my father's been telling you about Rodney,' she said, her indignant tongue stumbling on the words. 'But I assure you I am going to marry him.' She hesitated. 'What *did* Dad say?'

The stranger put his hands in his pockets and gazed at a point above her head. 'That your fiancé was a good-looking chap who played a very decent game of golf.'

Laura frowned at the exaggerated accent. 'That's all?'

'No. If memory serves, he also used the words 'smart', 'serious' and 'stuffy'. Something about his disapproving of the Cinnamon Arms. Which is where I met your father, by the way.'

'It would be,' said Laura gloomily — and then, forgetting that her family affairs were none of this extraordinary man's business, 'It's not that Dad drinks that much really, but since he retired from the bank he goes there to talk to friends and pass the time. Lately, since her husband died, he's been taking our neighbor along too.'

'Mrs de Vere? Yes, I met her. Your father is seeing her home. So I came on ahead.'

'Why?' asked Laura faintly.

'Why what?'

'Why did you come?' Laura saw no point in pretending his company delighted her.

'To eat, as a matter of fact. Your father invited me to dinner.'

'He wh — ? Oh, no!' She glanced, horrified, at the stove, from which came a doubtful smell and ominous sizzling noises. 'You shouldn't have distracted me . . . ' She made a dive for the door of the oven and yanked it open.

Inside, a pan of something which might once have been white was firing spitballs of butter at the walls. Laura seized a pair of oven mitts from a drawer, pulled out the pan, and dumped it on top of the stove. Totally ignoring the interloper, who didn't, after all, seem to pose much of a threat, she picked up a fork and began to prod doubtfully at what was meant to be flaky baked halibut.

'Maybe fish pie,' she muttered under her breath. 'That's about the best we can hope for.'

'I like fish pie.' Behind her she heard the scrape of a chair, and the sound of a solid body settling into it.

'Rodney doesn't.' Laura sighed and turned stricken blue eyes on the man who had made disaster inevitable. To be fair, she had forgotten the fish in the first place, but if he hadn't turned up at precisely the wrong moment she might have been in time to resuscitate the remains.

'To hell with Rodney.' He spoke with an edge to his voice that hadn't been there before. 'He'll eat your fish pie and like it.'

'He won't,' said Laura with certainty. 'At least, he may eat it, but . . . ' Her voice trailed off.

'But he'll complain? So what? It was an accident.'

'I know. But you don't know Rodney.'

The stranger hooked his arms over the back of a white wooden chair. 'No, and I'm not sure I want to.'

Laura lifted her chin, almost literally feeling her hackles rise. 'Rodney is my fiancé,' she informed him. 'And he's a good, sensible man.' Then, realizing how prissy that sounded, she added reluctantly, 'It's just that — well, sometimes I forget things, and he does get a little impatient.'

In fact he often got more than a little impatient, she was obliged to acknowledge to herself. But she wasn't about to admit that to this maddening intruder.

Almost four years had passed now since the evening Rodney Fosdyke, Cinnamon Bay's only accountant, had first cast an eye on her, Laura Allan, daughter of Lancelot Allan, retired bank manager of this seaside parish. And lately Rodney had begun to suggest that as he was now well-established in his business, it was time they set a date for their wedding. Laura had agreed, but with a reluctance she didn't altogether understand. After all, she had accepted Rodney's proposal because she was crazy about the tall, dark man whose attention had so flattered the shy young girl she had been. The girl who had never had a serious boyfriend. So why, when it came to setting a date, had she found herself mumbling excuses about not being convinced Ethan would be able

11

to look after her father, who wasn't used to managing on his own?

Rodney had said unsympathetically that a healthy dose of responsibility would do her feckless brother a power of good — a judgement Laura couldn't dispute.

Now, watching the nameless stranger sprawled beside her well-scrubbed kitchen table, with his black eyes watching her every move, it occurred to Laura, with a feeling of bewildered distress, that she was really in no hurry to get married.

'If you're staying to dinner, you'd better tell me your name,' she said abruptly and without the gentle courtesy she normally extended to the guests her gregarious father not infrequently collected from the Arms.

Before the stranger had a chance to answer, the front door slammed, and immediately afterwards a tuneless baritone began to warble, ''Rock of ages, cleft for me, let me hide myself in Thee.''

Laura sighed. Her father was home. If only he *had* hidden himself in church today instead of in the Cinnamon Arms, this disturbing man wouldn't be in her kitchen now looking confident, amused and, she supposed, ready to eat a good home-cooked meal. She stared disgustedly at the overcooked fish as Pal's tail thumped a lazy welcome to his master.

A few seconds later, a man with a clipped white moustache appeared in the doorway, glanced at the stranger, and gave a quick nod of approval.

Laura looked at her father with resignation. At sixty-five, Lancelot Allan carried himself with the taut, military bearing he had acquired during a stint in the army. He was still handsome in a dignified, silver-haired way. Handsome and utterly impossible, thought his daughter wryly.

'Ah,' Lancelot said now, nodding his satisfaction. 'See you and Adam have met. Everything in order, Laura?'

'We haven't met,' said Laura. 'And

absolutely nothing is in order.'

'Splendid, splendid. Glad to hear it.' Not for nothing had Lancelot spent a lifetime successfully ignoring customer complaints. It was a talent he still made the most of.

'Dad, this — this *gentleman* and I have not been introduced,' persisted Laura, determined to make her father face the facts. 'And we're having fish pie.'

'Good, good. Like fish pie. So does Ethan.'

'Rodney doesn't,' said Laura, wondering if she was slowly going mad. 'And I'd like to know — '

'My name's Adam Veryan,' interrupted a deceptively mild voice. 'Is there anything else you'd like to know, Miss Allan?'

Laura swung round and leaned against the counter for support. 'Adam — not *the* Adam Veryan? The war correspondent?' She tried desperately not to look impressed.

'Mmm. None other, I'm afraid.' He

sounded offhand and mildly bored, not at all as though he took his fame for granted. Her opinion of him rose half a notch.

'Oh. I've read some of your stories,' she admitted grudgingly. 'In the papers.'

'Have you?' His legs seemed to grow another few inches as he tilted his chair back and smiled. 'How encouraging. A woman who reads the papers *and* makes me fish pie.'

Was he laughing at her? Probably. He seemed to be the sort of man who laughed at everything, including accidental fish pie. Which reminded her: if she didn't get on with it, there wouldn't be any pie, accidental or otherwise.

She assumed her best repressive scowl and, turning her back on both men, began to busy herself with potatoes, onions and cheese. By the time everything was assembled, Lancelot had borne Adam off to have a drink.

Adam Veryan, thought Laura, slicing abstractedly into an onion which turned out to be her finger. That maddening, obstructive man was Adam Veryan, the insanely courageous reporter whose slogan was reputed to be, 'Find war, will travel.' In a world where wars erupted with predictable regularity, Mr Veryan had never, to her knowledge, been out of work.

Laura sluiced her finger under the tap and went on slicing. Yes, she'd read about Adam Veryan all right, and been as awestruck by his escapades as every other armchair adventurer in the country. She supposed she ought to have recognized him at once — although his picture rarely appeared beside the stories he filed. The accompanying photographs were much more likely to be of the battles and rebellions he covered, along with their aftermath of devastation, heroism and grief. For all his personal glamor, Adam Veryan saw no glamor in warfare. She knew that from the articles he wrote. She also knew that sometimes the heroism had been his. But he didn't write about that. Once he had single-handedly rescued three trapped civilians from a burning building. And he had even been taken hostage once or twice. But always he had managed to escape from danger with his magnificent body unscathed. Until the last time. Laura paused with her hand on a potato. He'd been wounded that last time, when he'd moved too close to the action and collected a stray bullet in the leg. Somewhere in — Africa, was it? Or the Middle East?

She shrugged. Wherever it was, Adam's wound obviously hadn't slowed him down for long. She hadn't even noticed a limp.

Shaking her head, Laura pressed doggedly on with her fish pie. Imagine meeting Adam Veryan here in Cinnamon Bay — and falling flat on her nose at his feet.

She started to giggle, and then decided it wasn't funny after all. It might have been if the man hadn't turned out to be one of those oversexed, over-confident jerks who

— no. That wasn't fair. She didn't actually *know* he was oversexed. Just because his smile made her go warm all over, it didn't mean . . .

Then again, maybe it did.

'It's a good thing he's only here for the evening,' she remarked without conviction to Pal, who pricked up his ears and licked his lips in hopeful anticipation of food.

Laura decided to keep her thoughts firmly on the preparation of dinner. The intrepid correspondent who was now comfortably consuming whisky with her pipe-smoking father had stirred up more than enough trouble for one day.

Fifteen minutes later, just as she was heaving a sigh of relief and wiping her hands on her jeans, she heard the sound of brisk footsteps in the hall.

She glanced up. Rodney, dressed in a well-cut dark blue blazer, was standing in the doorway looking elegant. The classic perfection of his features was marred only by a disapproving frown.

'Who's that fellow who let me in?' he

demanded, stalking toward her. 'And how often have I told you not to wipe your hands on your clothes?'

'They are *my* clothes,' said Laura, for once not mumbling an apology. 'And his name's Adam Veryan. You may have heard of him. Dad found him at the pub.'

'He would,' muttered Rodney who, if he had heard of Adam, was obviously not disposed to be impressed. 'Honestly, Laura, you really must do something about your father — '

'What do you suggest?' she asked sweetly. 'He's a little old to keep locked in his bedroom.'

'Don't be ridiculous.' Rodney's gaze lit on the fish pie. 'And what's *that*? I thought we were having baked halibut.'

'We were. It got too baked. I — '

'Honestly, Laura,' he repeated. 'It really is time — '

'Is your name honestly Honestly Laura?' drawled an interested voice from behind them.

Laura whirled round. Adam was

draped against the doorframe with his thumbs hooked into his belt and his fingers flat against his stomach. His piratical eyebrows were raised in what might have been polite enquiry, but was undoubtedly pure provocation. If he'd been wearing a stetson, he'd have looked exactly like the bad guy from a western come to clear out the saloon.

She glanced at Rodney. He didn't look anything like Roy Rogers, Clint Eastwood, or Gary Cooper. In fact, she decided, he was perfect in the part of the bombastic but nervous saloon keeper who didn't much relish a shoot-out on his turf. Briefly, Laura wondered if she was the turf, then gave herself a quick mental shake when she remembered that Adam Veryan couldn't possibly be interested in a fight to the death over quiet Laura Allan from Cinnamon Bay. He was famous, successful, known to have a way with the ladies, and totally unlikely to set his sights on an ordinary little country girl like her. Well, not little exactly. She was tall. But not his type.

'No,' she said, seeing Rodney's face turn a mottled shade of crimson. 'I'm just plain Laura. This, Mr Veryan, is my fiancé, Rodney Fosdyke.'

'We've met,' said Adam shortly.

Laura prayed for patience and the strength to get through the evening. The instant antagonism between the two men was already cracking across the kitchen like silent gunfire. Which was crazy, because up until a few minutes ago they had never laid eyes on one another. She shook her head and started juggling pans on the stove.

'Adam is staying for dinner too. Dad invited him,' she explained to Rodney over her shoulder. 'And he likes fish pie.' Laura added that quickly, without pausing to think. Then wished she hadn't.

Rodney's face turned from crimson to purple. It didn't suit him. She had always liked his pale skin and smoothly dark good looks. But this glowering, furious Rodney was not the courteous, endearingly strait-laced businessman she had fallen in love with. Indeed, she hadn't suspected the existence of this Rodney until he had put the ring on her finger. Since then, she had made his acquaintance a little too often for comfort.

She watched as he fought to gain control of his temper in front of Adam. And succeeded.

'That's — er — interesting,' he murmured. Only the muscles moving in his throat betrayed that what he really meant was, And I hope it chokes him.

'Isn't it?' said Laura. She peered through the glass door of the oven. 'I think dinner's ready. I just have to set the table . . . '

'You mean it's not done yet?' Rodney managed to look as if she had just announced that they were to eat off the floor.

'No, I haven't had time . . . ' She stopped. Why was she making excuses? She'd already told him the table wasn't set.

'Allow me.' Adam reached over her shoulder as she scrabbled in a drawer for knives and forks. 'I'll fix it.'

'Thank you. The dining-room is second on the left.' As Adam loped out of the kitchen whistling a flat little tune between his teeth, Laura was left with the conviction that he had only made the offer in order to annoy Rodney. She had a feeling Adam didn't take kindly to exhibitions of masculine pomposity.

It wasn't until she turned round, after straining vegetables and removing the pie from the oven, that she realized the growling sounds coming from behind her were made not by Pal, but by Rodney.

Oh, dear. This was working up to be a very fraught meal.

But for a while, as the four of them sat down to eat in the oak-paneled dining-room with ivy trailing gently round the window, it looked as though they might get through dinner without a scene.

Rodney, his face tight and waxlike, concentrated on the food on his plate. Only a slight dilation of his nostrils indicated his unfavourable opinion of both the company and the pie. Lancelot sat upright at the end of the table processing his food with precision. Adam alone ate with evident appreciation, pausing now and then between bites to glance at Laura with what appeared to be amusement, and at Rodney with a certain caustic disbelief.

Laura ignored him and chatted brightly to her father, who grunted and said, 'Yes, my dear,' with comfortable and soothing regularity.

The trouble began when a boyish voice shouted from the hallway, 'Hi, people! I'm home. Dad, is it OK if I bring a few of the school pets home for the summer?' A lanky teenager with brown eyes and a lot of soft brown hair bounded through the doorway and sat down.

Laura looked up from her plate. 'I

thought you were eating at Tony's,' she said mildly.

'I already have. Is it OK, Dad? About the pets?'

Lancelot wiped his mouth with a napkin, snared a tomato on the end of his fork and grunted, 'Ask Laura.'

Rodney put down his knife and fork and gave the newcomer a look that ought to have reduced him to vapour. 'Don't be ridiculous, Ethan. Your sister has quite enough to do as it is. I've told you before — '

'Surely Laura can speak for herself?' Adam's quiet, authoritative baritone cut off Rodney's lecture in mid-stream. He gave his hostess a slow, contemplative smile before turning his attention to Ethan. 'We haven't met,' he said to the startled young man. 'I'm Adam Veryan. Your sister makes a most excellent fish pie.'

Laura felt her cheeks turning pink. 'I'll handle this,' she said quietly, seeing Rodney's fingers clench around his fork. Of course Adam was deliberately trying to cause trouble. It seemed to be the thing he did best. She turned to her father, who was extracting a fishbone from his teeth. 'Dad, what do you think?'

'Told you. Up to you, my dear.' Lancelot laid the bone carefully on the edge of his plate.

Laura sighed. Her father had been leaving things up to her ever since her mother had died when she was ten.

There had been housekeepers at first, of course, but they hadn't lasted long. Most of them, quite unreasonably according to Ethan, had taken hysterical objection to mice cavorting in the cupboards and frogs croaking in the kitchen sink. The last housekeeper had departed with an impressive display of dudgeon over the appearance of two baleful bats not, unfortunately, in the belfry but in the breadbox. After that Lancelot had been quite content to leave the housekeeping 'up to young Laura', who had padded around at weekends with a vacuum cleaner and mops and never tried to tidy up his slippers or throw away his collection of noxious pipes.

'Ridiculous,' she heard Rodney snap.

Adam's eyes flicked to his face. 'Oh, I don't know,' he drawled. 'I'm sure Laura can manage a few hamsters.'

'That's not the point,' began Rodney, rising at once to the bait. 'Laura — '

Laura turned to her brother. 'How many?' she asked, knowing she was being unwise. One false move and she could end up with a houseful of fauna. But she was damned if she was letting either of these bossy men tell her how she could, or couldn't, run her household.

'Four rabbits, sixteen gerbils and a guinea pig,' replied Ethan blithely.

'No,' said Laura.

A choking sound from Adam's side of the table grated across Laura's already fragile nerves. When he gibed softly, 'Afraid of little furry things, blue-eyes?' she wondered if she could discreetly salt his wine.

Rodney patted her hand and gave a

patronising smile. 'Of course she is,' he said loftily. 'Laura has a delicate constitution.'

Laura had always thought she had a particularly robust constitution. And she wasn't in the least afraid of fur.

'All right,' she said to Ethan. 'You can bring them home. But only for the summer.'

'Great. Thanks.' Ethan beamed at Laura and sent Adam a look of worshipful admiration.

It wasn't until she saw one of Adam's heavy eyelids droop in an exaggerated wink that Laura realized she'd been properly had. Rodney, in an attempt to assert his right to manage Laura's life, had fallen into the same trap she had. The suggestion that she was some feeble little wimp who couldn't make decisions for herself had pushed her into accepting Ethan's menagerie.

Damn Adam Veryan anyway. Because of him, baked halibut had become fish pie, and Rodney looked as if he was about to explode. On top of that, she was stuck with a houseful of fur for the summer. As if Pal and the two cats were not enough.

When her father started humming 'Onward Christian Soldiers', beneath his breath, she knew the evening could only get worse.

It did. Almost at once.

'Adam here needs a bed,' Lancelot announced abruptly. He went on humming.

Laura blinked. She could think of a lot of things Adam needed. A bed wasn't one of them. She said nothing, and started to pick up the plates.

Lancelot hummed another few bars. 'Mentioned our basement room,' he explained, when his gambit was met with unbroken silence. 'Matter of bed and breakfast. Just for a month or two. Wants peace and quiet to write his autobiography. Something to do while his leg's on the mend.' He cleared his throat and broke off a large piece of bread. 'Knew you'd be pleased, Laura. Being interested in history and all that.'

2

Vaguely, Laura wondered what 'history and all that' had to do with Adam and modern warfare. Then the import of her father's words sank in. With a heart-stopping thud.

'Peace and quiet? Here? Dad, that's crazy.' It was the only objection she could think of on the spur of the moment, but she hoped it would do.

'Humph. Been peaceful enough ever since we got rid of those damned housekeeping women.' Lancelot wasn't interested in objections.

'Yes, but Dad, the basement — well, it's not — I mean, I don't think it's a good idea.'

Adam rested his forearms on the table and gave her a smile that she supposed was meant to look martyred. In fact it looked lazy and sexy. 'No room at the inn?' he suggested, shrugging. 'Don't worry, it won't be the first time I've been asked to move on.'

'I'm not surprised,' muttered Rodney.

Neither was Laura. Although she didn't mind having house guests, Adam had proved he was one of those people who could disrupt things without even trying. He seemed to be a natural-born disturber of the peace. With his long, feral body and pirate's grin, he certainly disturbed *her* peace in a way that respectable, conservative Rodney never had.

'I'm sorry,' she said, standing up so quickly that she almost dropped the plates on the floor, 'but our basement really isn't suitable as an office — '

'Course it is,' said Lancelot. 'Nice big room with a desk, his own bathroom, big king-sized bed — '

'Sold,' said Adam, holding up his hand. 'I'll take it.'

'But — ' said Laura and Rodney in unison.

'Splendid,' said Lancelot, reaching for his pipe.

'Wow. Dynamic,' crowed Ethan.

'Laura has more than enough to do already,' Rodney pronounced, casting an immediate damper on the celebration. He sounded more grumpy than solicitous, but Laura was grateful for his support just the same.

'Nonsense,' said Lancelot. 'Just as easy to cook for four as three. Or five,' he added, with a significant look at Rodney's empty plate.

Adam stood up. All six foot forever of him. 'Will I be too much for you, Laura?' he asked, placing both fists on the table and bending toward her. His dark eyes met hers with a challenge so explicit it was impossible to ignore.

Laura pinched her lips together. He knew she found him disturbing. Did he also imagine she was going to be intimidated by a pair of bedroom eyes? Four years ago she would have been. *Had* been, on one memorable occasion. But not now. Now she was twenty-two going on twenty-three, and soon she would be married to sensible, reliable

Rodney. Of course this overpowering, overassured man wouldn't be too much for her. She wouldn't allow him to be.

'Dad's right,' she replied coolly. 'What's one extra mouth? And I'm sure you can make your own bed.'

'I'd rather you made it,' he said, removing the plates from her hands when, inexplicably, they started to shake.

It sounded innocent enough, the helpless male act. But Laura wasn't deceived for one moment.

'What did you mean by that?' she demanded, following him out of the room when she realized he was heading for the kitchen. 'I cook, I dust, I vacuum. I don't do beds. In any sense of the word.'

Adam lounged against the counter and crossed his arms. 'Don't you?' he said. 'We'll see.'

Laura bit her lip. Did he *have* to look like that? Almost like an invitation to — what? She shied away from the thought, and said quickly, 'Your leg.

There doesn't seem to be much wrong with it any more.'

'I'm sorry. Would you prefer it if I sported a limp?' His tone was dry as burnt toast.

'No, of course not.' Laura hadn't meant to sound unfeeling. 'I just wondered — '

'If I was malingering? No, Miss Allan, I am not. I was lucky enough to have a very skilled surgeon, but my doctor has advised me to stay away from battle lines for a month or two if I want to be free of future problems. Were you hoping to send me off to war?' His crooked smile delivered a subtle rebuke.

'Certainly not.' Laura was indignant. She might not like Adam, but she wouldn't want to send anyone off to war. She took a quick breath and squared her shoulders. 'I didn't mean that at all. I just thought you might have trouble with the stairs.'

'Did you?' he drawled.

'Yes, I . . . ' No, she hadn't. And he

knew it. 'Would you like to see the room before you make up your mind?' she finished lamely, feeling embarrassed, contrite and supremely irritated with the cause of her discomfort.

'Nope. My mind's already made up. I seldom change it.' His dark gaze settled on her face in a way that made Laura wonder if he expected her to come with the room, along with the desk and the bed. Then she remembered that he knew she was an ordinary small-town girl, engaged to a small-town accountant. All right, so it was her dreams — no, not dreams, surely, just her imagination — running away with her again. She must have been studying too hard.

'Wouldn't you find it easier to write in your own home?' she suggested, knowing she was grasping at straws.

'My home in Vancouver is currently occupied by my sister and four — no, make that five — engaging but obstreperous brats. Ann doesn't do husbands. At least not for long. In between them she moves in with me.'

'Your parents?' Laura suggested. 'Why not stay with them?'

'Difficult. They died in an accident at the ripe old age of seventy when they decided to take up ballooning. They said life was becoming too tame for them.'

Laura choked back the conventional words of sympathy that immediately sprang to her lips, because Adam was openly grinning. He was actually proud that his enterprising parents had gone out in a mad blaze of glory while attempting to spice up their lives. No wonder he had grown up a risk-taker. It obviously ran in the genes. Along with a healthy dose of insanity.

'I'm sorry to hear that,' she said formally, when convention finally won out.

'Don't be. My parents always lived on the edge. They liked it that way.'

Yes, that was what Laura had figured. And between the two of them, those parents had reared a daughter who didn't do husbands, and a son who had a passion for danger.

But she didn't need danger in her life.

Adam was watching her closely. 'If you were about to suggest a cosy little hideaway in Siberia or the Sahara, don't,' he said drily. 'I've decided to write my book here. I like the atmosphere.'

'Atmosphere?'

'Mmm. Sea, sand and memories. Some of them good ones.' He smoothed a hand over his jaw, which showed signs of five o'clock shadow.

Memories? Laura wondered what sort of memories, but after one look at the discouraging line of his mouth she made up her mind not to ask.

'The hotel,' she persisted, without much hope. 'What's wrong with renting a room there?'

'Nothing much. I just happen to prefer bed and breakfast.'

There was that white, incendiary smile again. Laura was about to tell him he could forget both the bed *and* the breakfast when she saw his eyes flicker, and knew someone had followed them into the kitchen. Before she could move, with slow deliberation Adam had curved his right hand round the back of her neck.

She gasped as if she'd been winded. The touch of his fingers on her skin sent instant heat quivering down her spine. Heat that had nothing to do with the warmth of a June evening. She swayed toward him, mesmerised by the dark lights in his eyes.

'Laura! What on earth ... ?' Rodney's voice shattered the moment like a rock hurled through a window.

Laura gave a strangled moan and spun round to face the accusing glare of her fiancé.

'Rodney, I ... ' She swallowed. Stammered, unconvincing excuses wouldn't work. *Shouldn't* work. Rodney would be entirely justified in imagining the worst. And if she wasn't mistaken, the worst was exactly what Adam meant him to imagine.

Her suspicions were confirmed when her unwanted guest looked Rodney's elegant figure up and down and drawled, 'What's it to be, Fosdyke? Pistols at dawn, or a civilised chat over a drink?'

'Adam!' Laura was aghast. 'There's no question of . . . ' She caught a glimpse of Rodney's pale, furious face. 'You'd better leave,' she said brusquely to Adam. 'Before — '

'Before your boyfriend attempts to defend your honour, and finds himself laid out on the floor? Maybe you're right.' His tone was flippant, but the set of his jaw convinced her he was quite capable of carrying out the threat.

Rodney's jaw tightened as well. When he started to raise his fists, all at once Laura saw red. 'Stop it!' she said furiously to Adam. 'Who do you think you are, pawing your way in here like some prize stallion with a right to every female in the herd? Rodney is the man I'm going to marry. And you're the one likely to find yourself on the floor. So please get out.'

Adam raised his eyebrows and shook his head at her as if she were an impertinent child who had stepped out of line. 'I was merely demonstrating to Fosdyke that he takes you too much for granted,' he said repressively. 'I am not in the habit of appropriating other men's property. Nor am I greatly attracted to very young women who haven't learned how to mind their tongues. So for the time being I'll try to keep my mating instincts in check.' He gave her cheek a condescending pat as he brushed past Rodney, whose fists remained clenched at his sides, and sauntered over to the door.

'I am nobody's *property*,' Laura practically spat at his back. 'And *I'm* not remotely attracted to arrogant, patronising men who . . . ' She caught sight of Rodney's face, and broke off.

It was the colour of putty. She felt a quick tug of remorse. Damn Adam Veryan. He might be as seductive a specimen of virility as had been seen in Cinnamon Bay since Miss Rogers from the school had married that handsome travel agent from the States — but he was also the rudest, most overbearing man she had ever met. Whereas Rodney, disapproving and critical as he often was, had been her rock and her support for the past four years.

Vaguely, and not for the first time, a notion brushed at the back of Laura's mind that a woman who had brought up Ethan and coped with Lancelot Allan since she was a child was hardly in need of any rock. But she pushed the thought away, wouldn't even consider it. Her mother had abandoned her rock. She, Laura, could not abandon Rodney without coming perilously close to following in Leah Allan's footsteps.

No, she had given her promise to Rodney, and promises weren't made to be broken. She owed him her loyalty, her trust and her love. The same devotion that, in spite of everything, her father had given to her mother.

She raised her head, smiled at her scowling fiancé, and placed a tentative hand on the sleeve of his expensive blue blazer.

He flinched as if her touch was repulsive.

'I'm sorry,' she murmured, not sure what she was sorry for, but understanding that his feelings needed soothing.

'I should hope so,' he said, stepping backwards and out of her reach. 'You'll have to learn to behave better than that, Laura, if you hope to be the next Mrs Fosdyke.'

'But it wasn't my . . . ' She stopped. No, it wasn't her fault. But she *had* responded to Adam, who was quite right that Rodney took her for granted. Ever since he had placed the ring on her finger, Rodney had treated her, not as an independent woman, but as a Fosdyke asset. And it had slowly become obvious that he felt the next Mrs Fosdyke needed a good deal of licking into shape. Laura touched the diamond she had worn for nearly three years. Had it really lost some of its lustre? Or was her imagination over-working again?

'I don't like Adam either,' she assured Rodney, deciding there was no point in making excuses for something that hadn't happened. She took a deep breath. 'As a matter of fact I find him thoroughly obnoxious.'

'Hmm.' Rodney looked very slightly mollified. 'I'm glad to hear you have *some* sort of taste.' He folded his hands solemnly on his stomach.

Laura supposed she ought to feel gratified. What she actually felt was irritated, and then guilty in case she wasn't being fair. Did he mean she had very little taste in anything else? She thought about asking for clarification, then decided not to. Rodney did have some reason to feel resentful.

Her instinct proved right. A few minutes later, after clearing his throat several times, he suggested a trip to Nanaimo to take in a new string quartet. She agreed, and they left the house quickly. Lancelot was asleep in front of the TV set, and Pal was asleep on his feet. Adam, much to Laura's relief, had disappeared, presumably to collect his luggage. She told Ethan to show him his room when he came back, and resolved to put the embrace that hadn't quite happened out of her mind.

She enjoyed the quartet. It was pleasant to sit in the dark, listening to music, and not having to make conversation. But Rodney must have used the time to review his options, because later on, as they sat over a quiet drink in a dignified hotel with a lot of damask, he informed her gravely that she was to begin preparations for their autumn wedding at once. 'Since you don't seem to have enough to do with your time,' he explained with a tight little smile.

Laura, for once, was speechless.

★   ★   ★

A raccoon's bespectacled face peered out from the branches of a birch tree at the bottom of the garden as Laura hurried across the grass the following morning. She smiled, and glanced back at the house, half expecting to see Adam at one of the windows. But there was no sign of him, and the only movement came from the ivy rippling in green waves across the stucco. She was glad her new boarder had elected to sleep in. His inflammatory presence wouldn't have added to her enjoyment of breakfast.

She stepped on to the path leading through the woods that were her most direct route to work, and the raccoon nattered softly and disappeared. Laura tilted her head back and sniffed the clean pine smell of early morning. She would miss this peaceful neighborhood when she married Rodney. Perhaps he was right that it was time to set a date . . . But oh, if only she could go to college first, complete her degree now that Ethan was older and her father had

Primrose for company . . . She kicked glumly at a small pebble in her path. There was no point even dreaming about college. Rodney said she could go on taking courses by correspondence if she must, but that he wanted his wife at home housekeeping and raising a family. As she had, for so many years, housekept for her father and Ethan.

The difference was that she *liked* looking after her father and her brother.

Laura stopped in her tracks. What was she thinking? Didn't she *want* to look after Rodney? Yes, of course she did. In a way. It was just that Rodney was a young and supposedly modern man, who ought to be able to do a few things for himself . . .

But Rodney wanted an heir to the Fosdyke name. Almost at once. And he wasn't used to doing for himself.

Laura sighed and unsnagged her blue overall from a bramble. Somehow she couldn't see Rodney with children. Adam, though . . . No. She wasn't going to think about Adam. Not when the sun was shining, the trees were green and sweet-scented, and she could see the soft bob of a deer's tail behind the bushes.

Twenty minutes later she pushed open the door of the bakery and breathed in the warm smell of bread.

'You look like a bleached bedsheet,' remarked her co-worker, Charlene, rudely shattering Laura's bucolic mood. 'You and Rodney have a night on the tiles?'

'String quartet,' said Laura, shaking her head. 'Rodney doesn't approve of tiles.'

'Do you want him to?' Charlene turned away and started rearranging rolls on the shelves.

'No, not really.' Laura stared at her friend's expressive back. It seemed unusually tense. 'Why do you ask?'

'No special reason.' Charlene swung round and gave Laura a big, vague smile. 'Jerry's made cheese bread today.'

Jerry, the baker who owned the store,

made cheese bread every day. Laura frowned, puzzled, and went into the back to wash her hands.

The morning passed quickly. There were more customers than usual, and the two young women were kept busy stocking shelves, filling bags and boxes, and assuring beady-eyed ladies that yes, the donuts were fresh-baked that morning. Jerry, emerging from the back now and then, did his best to slow down production by telling them not to do whatever they were doing the way they were doing it — but they were used to Jerry, and paid him very little attention.

Finally, a few minutes after noon, there was a break in the traffic. Laura leaned on the counter and wiped the back of her hand across her forehead. 'Thank goodness,' she said. 'Maybe now we'll get a chance to breathe.'

But when she looked up from a tray of cinnamon buns and found herself staring straight into Adam Veryan's mocking eyes she discovered breathing wasn't an option after all.

The faded jeans and the turtleneck were gone. In their place, he wore a pair of well-fitting gray trousers and a white silk shirt left open at the neck to reveal a promising hint of corded strength beneath.

Laura moistened her lips. 'What are you doing here?' she demanded.

'Pursuing the breakfast you didn't make me. I'll have two butterhorns and a cup of coffee. And what on earth have you done to your beautiful hair?'

He appeared to have totally forgotten yesterday's confrontation, along with his own brutally dismissive words.

For a moment, Laura couldn't find her voice. Then she shook off her unexpected paralysis and replied as though it wasn't important, 'I didn't fix your breakfast because you weren't up, and I don't make wake-up calls to jerks. Dad was supposed to tell you to help yourself.' When Adam gave her a narrow smile and said nothing, she added grudgingly, 'You can have two butterhorns, if you like, but we don't serve coffee. And Health Department regulations don't permit loose hair.'

'The Health Department doesn't know what it's missing,' said Adam, reaching for the gold barrette that held her flaming locks in a neat coil on top of her head.

'Don't . . . ' she began.

It was as far as she got, because at that moment a man's brisk voice from the doorway said, 'Laura, I've decided — ' and then snapped off in mid sentence. There was a long, electric pause. 'Laura, *what*, may I ask, is going on?'

'Hello, Rodney,' said Laura. She wondered why her heart had started thumping. 'Nothing's going on. I — um — I thought you were going home to have lunch with your mother.'

'Mother is out,' said Rodney stiffly. 'I — '

Adam, whose lazy-lidded gaze had been moving interestedly between Rodney and Laura, interrupted in a heavily sympathetic tone, 'Mom not home to make our lunch today? Bad show, that.'

Rodney glared at him. 'I don't believe my luncheon arrangements are any of your damned business,' he replied.

Adam's eyes glinted. 'Eloquently put,' he murmured. 'I see the accounting profession has a bright new star on its horizon. Naturally I wouldn't dream of interfering with your — er — luncheon arrangements.'

Laura caught Charlene's eye and smothered a smile. What was this, a contest to see who could out-pompous whom?

Suddenly Rodney descended from his high horse with unpompous speed. 'What the devil are you doing here anyway?' he demanded.

Adam shrugged, and hitched a hip on the counter.

'He came for breakfast,' said Laura quickly, deciding it was time to defuse this volatile situation before it got out of hand.

'Breakfast? I thought you were providing the fellow with breakfast at home.'

Rodney, frowning his disapproval, rounded on her at once.

'I left instructions for Adam to help himself,' Laura explained, frowning too, because Adam's breakfast had nothing to do with Rodney. 'But apparently he didn't.'

'Laura, that is no way to run a bed-and-breakfast,' Rodney reproved her — and Laura, at last, got the picture.

Rodney's indignation was mainly directed at Adam. But Adam was an impossible target. He wouldn't stand still and allow himself to get hit. So Rodney was taking out his frustrations on the fiancée he perceived as easy game. And at one time he would have been right.

Not any more. All at once Laura had had enough. 'I am not running a bed-and-breakfast, this is a bakery not a fencing parlour, and you can both go and sharpen your swords someplace else. *Out*.' She roared the last word like a drill sergeant with a mission to deafen.

Rodney started, but neither man moved.

Laura drew a deep breath. 'I said out,' she repeated.

Still nobody moved, so Laura gritted her teeth and added, '*Please.*'

Rodney only glared and turned pinker, but Adam unhitched his hip from the counter, nodded, and said evenly, 'That's better. On second thoughts, I think I'll pass on the butterhorns. See you later, blue-eyes.' Swinging past Rodney as if he weren't there, he strolled out on to the street.

Laura watched him go. She'd never known a man who moved like that before. Not as Rodney did, with neat, efficient steps, but with a relaxed, easy swagger that reminded her of a tiger in slow motion. And yet he seemed to get where he was going just as fast.

When she saw that Rodney was watching her watching Adam, she turned hastily to help incoming customers.

Only once during the next half-hour

did she even look at her fiancé, and when she did, she saw that he was deep in conversation with Charlene, who looked more animated than Laura had seen her in weeks.

Rodney left the shop a short time later with a curt goodbye to Laura and a much friendlier one to Charlene. Laura felt guiltily glad that she had made no arrangement to meet him later. After the stand-off in the bakery, any meeting was bound to be a strain.

To her relief, there was no sign of Adam when she arrived home from work that evening. She was in no mood for another encounter with a man whose very presence was a provocation.

As soon as supper was over she decided that what she needed was fresh air and a peaceful stroll on the beach to soothe her nerves, so she changed into denim shorts and whistled for Pal, who was catching up on his sleep on Ethan's bed.

A few minutes later the two of them were scrambling down the steep path which started at the end of the road and wound its way through a tangle of scruffy bushes to the beach.

It was deserted, as she had hoped, and Laura drew a long breath of satisfaction.

Alone, enfolded in the warmth of a fading summer afternoon, it was impossible not to let the waves washing gently on to the sand wash the cares of the day away too. She gazed dreamily at the soft purple outlines of the islands, while Pal bustled to the edge of the ocean to watch for non-existent fish.

Peace, she thought, sinking on to a sea-bleached log as a small breeze blew her hair across her face. Just sand and wind. No cares, no confusion — no Rodney and Adam.

But when she pushed the hair out of her eyes she saw at once that her peace would be short-lived. On the far side of the bay a tall figure had appeared from behind a rock. As Laura watched, it paused for a moment, then began to move steadily toward her.

Adam, barefooted, bare-chested and wearing shorts that exposed his endless brown legs, had also sought solitude on the beach. Laura sighed. It seemed that both of them were doomed to disappointment.

'Good evening,' he said when he came up to her, inclining his head with unexpected formality.

Laura swallowed. Up close, his legs were as tough and muscular as an athlete's, and they were covered with a fine sprinkling of dark hair. There was also a small white scar just above his right ankle. She supposed that was all the evidence that remained of his wound.

'Good evening,' she mumbled.

Adam looked down at her with a glint in his eye that she found even more disturbing than his legs. Then after a while, and without saying anything further, he lowered himself on to the other end of the log and fixed his gaze on the horizon.

Immediately Laura started to scramble

up. But in her anxiety to escape from a danger she sensed but couldn't really define, her bare knees brushed up against his thigh. The contact sent an instant shockwave through her body, and she froze, momentarily unable to move. Then, as the electricity continued to sizzle, she began to wriggle backward along the log.

Adam turned his head and watched her for a few seconds before saying pensively, 'Mmm. You squirm very seductively, blue-eyes. But I think you'd better save it for Fosdyke.'

'Oh!' Laura gasped. 'Of all the conceited, vain, egotistical toads I've ever met! Do you really imagine I'd throw myself at *you*?'

To her fury, Adam only laughed, and swung a leg over the log. 'No. And even if you did, I'm not at all sure I'd take the time to catch you.'

'Of course you wouldn't,' scoffed Laura, devastated to discover that his laughing rejection of what hadn't been offered actually hurt. 'Because you're not attracted to very young women with sharp tongues. Any more than I'm attracted to middle-aged toads with big egos.'

'Ouch,' said Adam. 'Middle-aged? Keep it up, blue-eyes, and I may find myself obliged to do something about that tongue of yours after all.' He leaned forward, and although he made no move to touch her, Laura felt as if her skin had just been scorched.

She jumped to her feet. 'Adam,' she said much too loudly, 'my tongue is not your concern. And you're not doing anything about it. It may have escaped your notice, but I'm engaged to Rodney.'

'Oh it hasn't escaped my notice. And I admire your loyalty.' Adam's voice was suddenly as deadpan as his face. Only a muscle pulling at the corner of his mouth told her his admiration was liberally laced with amusement.

She frowned. 'Then why won't you go away and leave me in peace?'

'Because I'd rather stay here and

watch the sunset. But you can leave if you like.' His smile was bland but inflexible.

Laura swallowed. He looked so maddeningly delectable sitting there with his long brown legs straddling the log, and his dark eyes daring her to stay, but not much caring if she didn't, that she was forced to admit, if only to herself, that she didn't really want to leave either.

'Is that why you came down here?' she asked, successfully skirting the issue. 'To watch the sunset?'

'Mmm. Partly. I've also been thinking.'

'About what?'

He shrugged and gave her a lazy look through his thick eyelashes. 'Oh, among other things, about why an intelligent girl like you got herself engaged to a humorless jackass like Fosdyke.'

Laura bristled. 'Rodney is not a jackass, he's very bright. And he's not . . . ' She had been going to say, 'he's not humorless,' but changed it to,

'And he laughs quite often.'

'Everybody laughs. Especially if the joke's on someone else. That doesn't mean they have a humorous bone in their bodies.'

Laura, irritated because she had a feeling he was right, said haughtily, 'Rodney also happens to be a gentleman. He once rescued me from someone just like you.'

Instead of being crushed, Adam laughed. 'Good for him. And was the someone suitably chastened?'

'Yes,' said Laura, who wasn't anxious to admit that she had needed rescuing from the clutches of the least desirable man in Cinnamon Bay. Known locally as Larry the Lecher, Larry Lovejoy had never been remotely like Adam, who was still grinning as if she'd told him a good joke.

'Anyway my engagement is none of your business,' she said, remembering, belatedly, that it wasn't.

'Perhaps not,' agreed Adam. He stood up. 'In any case, I don't propose to waste any more of my time discussing your deadly fiancé.'

'Rodney's not deadly.' Laura's reply was automatic.

Adam gazed up at the soft clouds scudding across the orange-tinted sky. 'OK, I'll rephrase. I don't mean to waste any more of my time discussing your fine upstanding suitor.' He turned away abruptly and began to stride across the sand. 'Come and get your feet wet,' he called to her over his shoulder. But he didn't stop to see if she was obeying.

Laura watched the muscles ripple across his back as the setting sun touched his skin with its fire. Adam might be a toad, she thought gloomily, but he was also an achingly beautiful man. Suddenly she wanted very much to stand beside him in the water, to feel that tough, bronzed skin against her own. Her heart began to beat like a drum, and she knew she ought to turn and walk away. But if she did, he would probably think she was just some little country chicken intimidated by the sophisticated world correspondent.

She didn't want him to think that. Nor, she discovered to her confusion, did she actually want to walk away.

She wanted to stand with her feet in the water and watch the sunset with Adam.

After only a moment's hesitation, she kicked off her sandals and followed him down to the sea.

For a few seconds he ignored her. Then, as she stared straight ahead, she felt his fingers forcing up her chin. Their eyes met. His were enigmatic, a little hard. Hers, she was very much afraid, were wide and anxious. Adam shook his head, as if in exasperation, and ploughed ahead through the waves. Flecks of spray sparked off his skin like diamond darts, and to Laura's bedazzled eyes he was Neptune rising from the deep. She waded after him, and in a few moments, with Pal barking excitedly from the shore, she was standing beside Adam as the ocean rose gently to her thighs.

She stared down at the distorted image of her toes beneath the water and felt a most urgent need to break what seemed to her an uncomfortable silence. It was a need that Adam apparently didn't share.

'What really brought you to Cinnamon Bay?' she asked, because it was the first thing that came into her mind. 'You could have written your story anywhere in Canada.'

Adam didn't answer at once, and when she looked up, she saw that he was frowning. 'You're a perceptive young lady,' he told her, but not as if he were paying her any compliment.

When he made no further comment, Laura said flatly, 'You're not going to answer me, are you?'

He shrugged. 'Why not? What do you want to know? That I came to Cinnamon Bay to lay a ghost?' His voice was level enough, but she detected a faint undertone of derision.

'Did you?' Having got this far, Laura

saw no reason to back off. Even though some ghosts were better left undisturbed. Especially the ghosts of lost lovers. And there was something about Adam's eyes . . .

'Yes,' he said, uncannily picking up her thoughts. 'It was a woman. Her name was Christine. Still is, I suppose. She married my sister's first husband.'

'Oh.' Laura fixed her gaze on a piece of seaweed caught between her toes, then asked awkwardly, 'Do you — do you want to talk about her?'

'Not particularly. Do you?'

That annoying glint was in his eye again, and Laura refused to be drawn. 'Not unless you do,' she replied, keeping her tone deliberately light. 'Shall we go home now?'

'Do you want to?' He draped a careless arm around her waist, and Laura suspected it was done, not because he was trying to make a pass, but because he was curious to see her reaction.

She glanced up, confused and horribly flustered. His fingers were playing lightly across her hip. But he was staring out to sea, and she couldn't be sure if he was aware of what he was doing to her or not. She decided that maybe he wasn't. In fact he seemed so abstracted that she wondered if he did need to talk but, man-like, wouldn't admit it.

She pushed away his arm, and stepped back. Adam began to strum his fingers on his thigh. His bare thigh.

'Yes. Yes, we'd better be going,' she said, gulping. And then, mostly to take her mind off his thighs, 'Um — Christine. The ghost you came to lay — '

He spun round so suddenly that the sea swirled up and soaked the bottom of her shorts. 'Ah, yes. But ghosts are so intangible, aren't they? And rarely willing to be laid.' He raised his devil's eyebrows in a way that she knew was intended to throw her off balance. But why, *why*, when he had all but admitted she didn't interest him, did he persist in taunting her with his subtly suggestive barbs? Did he get some perverse pleasure out of making her blush? As she knew very well she was now . . .

She lowered her eyes, and Adam laughed softly and dropped a hand on to her shoulder. Her confusion increased, and she was tinglingly conscious of the warmth of his fingers through her blouse and — was it her imagination, or was his thumb gently teasing her neck?

She raised her eyelids reluctantly. Adam's gaze was bright and a little hard — and Laura had a feeling this was some sort of test. The famous correspondent playing games with the inexperienced small-town girl who had dared to call him a toad. Which he was. When he placed his free hand on her other shoulder, she stepped back and flung herself indignantly sideways without pausing to see where she was putting her feet. The left one landed on a bulb of slippery seaweed.

She stumbled and threw up her arms, flailing them like an out-of-control windmill. Then she felt herself falling. The islands revolved in slow motion and seemed to tip upside down.

She came to rest with her face in the water and the incoming tide washing gently over her head.

At once she struggled on to her elbows, wet, coughing, and crimson-faced. When she was able to see again, she found that Adam was standing over her with his hands on his hips and a gleam of outright devilment in his eyes. But he wasn't actually laughing. Laura supposed she should be thankful for that.

She wasn't thankful. She was embarrassed, angry, soaked, and damned if she was going to ask him for help. Shifting on to her knees, she started to heave herself upright. And capsized when a wave larger than the others broke foaming into her face.

Spluttering, she struggled up for the second time, and felt two strong arms grab her under the arms.

'I can manage . . . ' she began. Then decided to save her breath because

Adam was holding her dripping body against his chest with one powerful arm, and her feet had already left the ground. His dangerously seductive lips were only a few inches from her own. He smelled warm and male and enticing, and she knew he would taste of spice and salt.

Except that he wasn't for her to taste.

She closed her eyes and turned her face so that it was buried against his shoulder — which didn't help much because his skin felt so much like smooth, strong silk that she longed to run her wet palms all over him, to stroke his back, his hips, the firm flat planes of his stomach . . .

'You'd better put me down,' she managed to gasp.

'No. I'd better get you back to the house. You're a charmingly damp armful, Aphrodite of the Sea, but it's getting chilly. We'll have to postpone the sunset, I'm afraid.'

'You can't postpone sunsets,' she mumbled into his shoulder. 'And if you'll just put me down, I'll get myself back to the house.' It *was* chilly, and the cold was beginning to restore her common sense.

'Why? Afraid I'll kiss you? I promise I won't.' His voice was low and mocking, but even so it sent ripples of excitement down her spine.

Laura didn't answer. What she was really afraid of was the possibility that *she* would kiss him.

Adam set her on her feet and gazed down at her. His eyes gleamed, as if he were contemplating further provocation, but after a moment his lips quirked almost imperceptibly and he said, 'Right. Come on, Pal. Let's go.' With practiced ease he swept Laura back into his arms and started to walk up the beach. When he came to the place where she had dropped her sandals, he draped her casually over his shoulder and bent down to scoop them up in one hand. 'OK?' he asked, continuing on his way.

Rather too OK, thought Laura,

knowing she ought to be putting up a fight, but instead letting her fingers trail slowly over Adam's back as, with Pal frisking beside him, he bore her in this undignified but undeniably stimulating position across the sands.

When they reached the path, he shifted her back into his arms. At that point Laura decided it was much too late to resist his caveman tactics, and gave herself up to the luxury of being carried home by a man who smelled good, felt good, looked good, and would give any of her historical heroes — Sir Walter Raleigh and Peter Abelard came to mind — a run for their money. And he would do it without getting any of his body parts lopped off.

It wasn't until they reached the gate in front of her house that Laura remembered she had a fiancé who, in his own way, was equally good-looking. And she only remembered then because Rodney was standing on the top step with his hands in the pockets of smart, gray flannel trousers, looking down at her as if he suspected she'd joined forces with the devil.

'Good evening, Laura,' he said, in a voice so controlled she expected it to snap. 'I suppose it's too much to ask for an explanation for this disgraceful exhibition?'

Just at this moment, it was.

Laura groaned, turned her head away, and buried her nose in the sinews of Adam's neck.

3

'The explanation ought to be obvious.' Laura, still trying to cope with this absurd turn of events, heard Adam's voice coming to her rescue. 'Laura had a fall. She's wet and she needs a change of clothes.'

Rodney ignored him. 'Can't you walk?' he demanded, as if only the weak and self-indulgent didn't use legs.

Laura decided it was time to get a grip on herself. 'Yes, I can,' she began. 'But — '

Adam interrupted. 'But I walk faster than she does. And my body heat helped to keep her warm.'

No, thought Laura. No, he didn't really say that. He wouldn't . . .

But of course she knew he'd said exactly that. Especially when she turned her head and saw that Rodney's face had turned an unappetising orange.

'You can put me down now,' she said firmly. 'But thank you for the ride. Rodney, how nice to see you. I didn't know you were coming.'

'Apparently,' snapped Rodney. 'And I wasn't. I changed my mind.'

Laura blinked. Rodney never changed his mind. And Adam hadn't put her down. He was right about the body heat, though. She did feel most unreasonably warm.

'I said put me down,' she repeated.

'So you did. Fosdyke, you'd better take over.'

Before she had time to protest, Adam was holding her out as if she were a damp and unwieldy parcel, and attempting to dump her in Rodney's reluctant arms. Rodney stepped hastily backwards, but in the ensuing scuffle Laura managed to end up on her feet. Belatedly realizing his obligations, her husband-to-be made an impatient but half-hearted grab to pick her up.

She dodged through the doorway. 'Will you two stop trying to pass me around like the Olympic flame?' she said irritably. 'Rodney, make yourself comfortable. I'll be down in a minute.'

She ran up to her room thinking dark thoughts about the idiotic behaviour of men in general and the two down below in particular.

Of course, now that she considered it — and Adam had made her consider it — Rodney had been becoming progressively more impossible as the months passed. He seemed to think a ring gave him the right to rule her life . . .

And then there was Adam. Laura shook her head, and gazed glumly at the unopened textbook on her desk. Adam was a different matter altogether. Adam didn't want to rule her life, he merely wanted to disrupt it. Or, if he didn't actually want to, disruption followed naturally in his wake. In fact he had given her more cause for confusion in two days than Rodney had done in two years. And she hardly knew how to think straight any more.

Feeling as if she'd been buffeted

between a sexy tornado and a hail-storm, Laura started peeling off her clothes. It wasn't until several minutes later, after she had slipped into dry white slacks and a yellow blouse, that she became aware of a change in the atmosphere of the house.

Lancelot was in the bath warbling 'Jerusalem' at the top of his voice. That was normal. But a curious squeaking noise that might have been a demented bagpipe was not. Nor were all the crashing sounds coming from the kitchen. Surely two supposedly mature men couldn't be indulging in fisticuffs among her pots and pans? Muttering under her breath, Laura ran a hand through the damp mat of her hair and hurried down-stairs to put a stop to whatever was going on.

When she reached the kitchen door she stopped dead.

On the white countertop she had earlier wiped clean were four cages containing varying shades of fur. The kind of fur that didn't keep still. In the first cage the demented bagpipe, who turned out to be a portly brown guinea pig. Two other cages were filled with woodchips from which, every now and then, the perky face of a gerbil came popping up. In the last cage, four black and white creatures were lifting mobile pink noses to sniff the air as their pink paws scrabbled at the wire that fenced them in.

On the kitchen table, beaming ecstatically, sat Ethan. Leaning against the window, his dark head framed in green ivy, stood Adam. Laura caught his eye, and his lips parted in the kind of smile that made her want to throw things at his head. She had to remind herself that she was too old for tantrums, however justified.

'Ethan,' said Laura, turning on her brother. 'You said rabbits. Those things with the noses and tails are not rabbits.'

Ethan raised ingenuous brown eyes. 'No,' he agreed. 'They're hooded rats. My teacher made a mistake. Their names are Aphrodite, Athena, Cassandra and

Demetrius. Aren't they cute?'

'They're not rabbits,' repeated Laura. When she heard a smothered chuckle from the direction of the window, she turned round to glare at Adam. 'This is all your fault,' she snapped.

'It most certainly is not. I refuse to be held responsible for your lack of willpower. You have only yourself to blame, blue-eyes.'

The fact that he was right didn't do a thing to lessen Laura's irritation. 'We can't possibly keep them all,' she told her brother.

Ethan's face fell as if she'd blotted out his sun, and she added crossly, 'We've nowhere to put them.'

'Nonsense,' said Adam, his eyes narrowing. 'Didn't you tell me you believe in keeping your promises?'

'Yes, but — '

'But you're annoyed with me for no good reason, so you're going to take it out on your brother. Think again, blue-eyes. The hooded ladies can go in the garage, the gerbils can live in

Ethan's bedroom, and I'll keep Howard in the basement with me. So don't let's hear any more objections.'

He had it all figured out. Not content with upsetting Rodney, Adam was trying to rearrange the way she ran her house. And as it *was* her house, she would definitely object all she liked.

She had her mouth open to do just that when she caught a glimpse of Ethan's face. It was alight with hero-worship. Laura saw nothing about Adam to worship, but she knew suddenly that the last thing she wanted was to come out of this mess looking like the wicked witch who had spoiled all the fun, while His Arrogance stole the show as hero of the day.

'Who is Howard?' she asked finally, when she had her voice sufficiently under control not to shout.

'The guinea pig.'

'Oh.' She squeezed her eyes shut, in the vain hope that when she opened them again the menagerie on the counter would have vanished, and

78

Adam would have turned into a rock. A large black one shaped like a rat.

But, when she looked again, the cages were still on the counter and Adam was a strong, dark man with a sexy smile.

A muffled exclamation made her turn.

Rodney, tired of waiting in the sitting-room, was standing in the doorway with an expression of stark horror on his face.

As Laura tried desperately to gather her scattered wits, she heard a disembodied voice from upstairs carolling something about, ''Our shelter from the stormy blast, and our eternal home'.' She lifted her eyes in supplication. Shelter from the stormy blast seemed unlikely to happen in this particular home, which just at this moment she wished could be anything but eternal. An immediate lightning bolt, preferably directed at Adam, would be more than welcome.

But the lightning bolt came in the

form of a sudden swoop across the kitchen by Rodney, who with very unRodneylike language grabbed Laura's arm and towed her into the hallway before she had quite taken in that he'd moved. Just before he pulled her into the sitting-room, she threw an anxious glance over her shoulder.

Adam had his hands in his pockets. He was watching their progress with interest, and there was a narrow, indecipherable smile on his lips. The next moment Rodney had closed the door sharply behind them.

'This,' he said belligerently, 'has gone far enough.'

'What has?' Laura rubbed her arm.

'Your Adam Veryan. You don't expect me to believe that zoo in the kitchen isn't his doing?'

It was, more or less. Adam's inflammatory presence at the table was what had pushed her into giving in to Ethan's plea. But she wasn't going to admit that to Rodney, especially as Adam was right about her deplorable lack of willpower. 'It's not Adam's fault,' she said reluctantly. 'I'm the one who gave Ethan permission to bring the school's animals home.'

'Rabbits,' muttered Rodney, his long fingers strumming on the back of the overstuffed gold and brown sofa. 'He said rabbits. I will not have my fiancée living in a zoo. It's not proper.'

'I don't think you have much choice,' said Laura, as gently as possible. There was no point in provoking Rodney further. 'The zoo is already here.' When she saw his face swell up like a pallid full moon, she placed a placating hand on his sleeve.

For a moment he glared down at it as if he'd like to squash it, then he mumbled something under his breath, said, 'Very well, Laura,' and to her intense surprise pulled her into his arms to deliver what felt like a possessive and carefully calculated kiss.

For a few seconds Laura resisted. Then she remembered that this was her fiancé, the man she was going to marry, and that he was kissing her with a thoroughness quite different from his normal reserved pecks. Yet this wasn't anything like the kisses she had read about in books. It was more than Rodney's usual restrained salute, but the earth wasn't moving for her. And the truth was, his lips felt cold and wet.

Probably all that earth moving stuff was wishful thinking, she decided with a small stab of regret.

Still, it was worth finding out, now that she had the opportunity. Clinging to his shoulders, she returned the kiss with an enthusiasm she couldn't truly feel.

What she did feel was Rodney's response. Instead of welcoming her embrace, he pushed her away roughly, said, 'Behave yourself, Laura,' and raised his hand as if he meant to slap her.

But at that moment a deep voice drawled softly through the open window, 'How very touching. Aphrodite and her Dionysius, I presume.'

'Aphrodite's a rat,' gasped Laura. She wasn't sure why it mattered, but she would have given a lot not to have been caught by Adam in what had started out as a perfectly acceptable embrace between two people who planned to get married, and ended in what might have turned into an ugly scene.

'Ah.' One of Adam's long legs appeared over the edge of the sill, and a moment later the rest of him swung smoothly on to the dusty beige carpet. 'And Dionysius is the god of wine and fertility. Hardly an apt comparison, I agree.' He turned to Laura, and there was something hard and personal in his look. 'But Aphrodite, I assure you, is no rat. Not if she looks the way you do.'

Laura, observing Rodney's face turn from sheet-white to violent crimson — it had done a lot of that lately — straightened her shoulders and said, 'I'm not susceptible to flattery, Mr Veryan, so you can save your breath.'

'And what makes you think that was flattery, Miss Allan?' replied Adam with an edge to his voice. 'In my opinion rats are interesting creatures.'

Laura didn't have time to say, 'Toads aren't,' because Rodney appeared to be choking.

'Laura, either this fellow leaves your house at once,' he spluttered, 'or . . . '

'Or what, Rodney?' Laura knew he had right on his side. After all, he hadn't actually slapped her, and maybe he wouldn't have, even without Adam's intervention. And Adam was an arrogant rogue who, perhaps without seriously intending to, was putting a huge strain on their relationship. But, greatly to her surprise, she discovered she didn't much care for ultimatums.

'Or I shall have to give serious thought to the matter of whether you will make me a suitable wife.' Rodney straightened his tie and looked at her as if he expected her to fall on her knees and beg forgiveness.

Adam crossed his arms and settled himself on the window-sill as if he were taking his place at a ball game.

'Adam, go away,' cried Laura. 'Rodney, I . . . '

Rodney raised his eyebrows. 'Well? Is he leaving?'

'Nope,' said Adam.

'Laura?' Rodney ignored him and gave Laura a thinly complacent smile.

A little too complacent and too thin, thought Laura distractedly. Did she *want* to stay engaged to Rodney?

Oh, but he'd been good to her in his way, respecting her virtue, instructing her in the ways of his world with a condescending but earnest dedication. She owed him something for all the years they had been together even if, lately, as she had grown older and more independent, he had grown more bombastic and dictatorial. It was wrong to break a promise just because some sexy pirate had erupted on to the scene to reinforce all her doubts about the future. Adam wouldn't stay. He wasn't even aware she was a woman, but looked on her as an ignorant small-town girl it was fun to tease. Adam, like all pirates, was into pillage and plunder and fast getaways. She was sure of it. And Rodney . . . Rodney was into account books, what the neighbors thought, and solid, uneventful respectability.

So could there be more than one choice?

Laura made the mistake of glancing across the room at Adam. He was still lounging on the sill with his arms crossed casually on his chest, and he returned her glance with a look so bright and mocking she felt as if a flame had seared her skin. Lord, the man was lethal.

And of course he had to go. How could there be any doubt?

'I don't — I mean it's not up to me,' she unaccountably heard herself explaining to Rodney. 'Dad's the one who invited Adam to stay.'

'It's always up to you,' said Rodney coldly.

Yes, of course it was. And Rodney hadn't been going out with her for four years without discovering that Lancelot almost always left the decision-making to her.

Adam began to whistle softly through his teeth.

'I don't know,' she began. 'It's — '

All of a sudden Rodney seemed to swell up and grow taller. And uglier. 'Very well,' he snapped. 'You never were much good at making up your mind, were you? I'll leave you to think about it.'

For a moment Laura thought he meant to try again to slap her. But instead he turned away, his lips pressed into a thin, flat line. He was practically out the door before she had the presence of mind to shake off her surprise and hurry after him.

'Wait,' she called. 'Rodney, I . . . '

But Rodney's neat gray Volvo was already halfway down the driveway, its wheels spinning unusually fast.

Laura waited until it was out of sight, and then, feeling as if the secure, solid earth she was used to had floated from under her feet, she turned to go back into the house. At the bottom of the stairs she paused, her shoulders drooping, and wrapped her arm around the polished mahogany stairpost.

What had happened to her and Rodney since the day when she had so joyfully accepted his ring? Their affectionate, if unequal, partnership had worked well enough at first. After a while a few cracks had begun to show. But these past few days their relationship seemed to have deteriorated into no more than a series of escalating confrontations.

Laura sighed. Who was she trying to fool? She knew very well what had happened. Adam had. And nothing had been the same since.

No, that wasn't fair. The truth was that even before Adam she'd had doubts. And firmly suppressed them. Then somehow Adam had forced all her uncertainties into the open with his careless charm and mocking black eyes.

Frowning, she placed a hand on the

rail and lifted her foot to climb the stairs. But before she had taken a step, a voice behind her said, 'Don't run away, blue-eyes. I want to talk to you.'

'I don't want to talk to you,' snapped Laura, not turning round. 'You've done enough damage already.' And if he called her blue-eyes once more, she would surely hit him.

'Too bad.' She felt her feet leave the floor as a brawny arm clamped around her thighs, and a moment later she was once again lying across his shoulder. This time it was covered in soft denim. A few seconds after that she had been deposited quite gently on a yellow print loveseat, and Adam was sitting beside her with his fist pressed into the cushions beside her waist. His face was only a few inches from her own.

She drew in her breath and leaned as far away from him as she could. His nearness frightened and inflamed her at the same time, and she was more conscious than ever of the dangerous power of his masculine appeal.

'Now,' he said, his warm breath teasing her skin as he reached up to remove the black ribbon from her hair. 'It's time you started facing facts.'

'About what?' Laura closed her eyes in a brief but vain attempt to shut him out.

'About Fosdyke, of course. If I hadn't decided to keep an eye on you, God knows what might have happened.'

'I didn't need your help,' she said quickly. 'Rodney wouldn't have hurt me. I wouldn't have let him. And I *am* going to marry him.'

'Are you sure?' The hand beside her waist moved slightly, and she felt it brush against her hip.

'Of course I'm sure.' Laura was surprised to learn how easily she lied. His touch was pure fire, even through the material of her slacks. 'And now — and now will you please let me go.' Inexplicably, tears came to her eyes. 'It's all because of you that Rodney left.'

'No. It's because of you, blue-eyes.

Sooner or later you have to come to terms with that.'

'There's nothing for me to come to terms with.' Laura sat up very straight, accidentally touching his leg. She jerked back as if she'd hit a live wire.

Adam, noting her reaction, smiled cynically. 'Isn't there?'

'No. No, there isn't.'

'Is that so?' His voice was low, rasping, hypnotic.

Laura gazed up at him, fascinated, and without meaning to she picked up his hand and laid it on her knee. Adam's eyes glittered darkly, and he slid his palm slowly up her leg. She was frozen, unable to move.

'Want me to stop?' he asked softly.

She tried to nod, but found herself shaking her head. Then, when she was sure he meant to explore the part of her that even Rodney had never touched, he drew his hand away, moved it behind her back and over the rounded tautness of her rear, stroking and arousing until her body could stand it no longer, and she cried out.

'Adam. Please . . . '

'You do want me to stop.' He sat up at once, but his hand still lay casually on her thigh and he was rubbing gently at the white fabric of her slacks.

She couldn't bear it if he stopped. But he must. This was her father's house — she could hear him humming in the distance — and she was engaged to Rodney.

'Yes,' she gasped. 'Yes, stop.'

He did, at once, and flung himself against the back of the loveseat. 'Well?' He raised a carelessly questioning eyebrow, just as if he hadn't, with a few moments of unbelievably sweet torture, disrupted all her previous notions about the relationship between a man and woman. 'Do you still insist you love Fosdyke?'

Laura shook her head. 'No. How can I? Rodney's never — I mean . . . ' She gave up because he was looking at her with the kind of stern compassion that told her the battle was already lost.

'You see,' he said, but not as if it gave him any pleasure. 'I told you you can't possibly marry him.'

Laura thought about that, forced herself to look beyond this man's dangerous but very temporary magnetism to the lifetime she had planned to spend with Rodney.

'I can,' she said slowly. 'I made him a promise. Rodney's been good to me in his own way. I met him because he was there when I needed him. Why should I betray his trust and let him down just because some sexy stranger has blown into town and wants to amuse himself with the first thing he sees in a skirt?'

'Slacks,' said Adam, unperturbed. 'And I'm flattered to know you think I'm sexy. But whatever gives you the idea that I want to amuse myself with you?'

Laura stared at a button on his shirt. It was coming loose. 'If you don't, you're even more of a toad than I thought,' she told him dully. 'No man with a shred of decency would try to

93

steal another man's woman just to prove he could.'

Adam leaned forward and caught a handful of her hair in his fist. 'I hate to shatter your illusions, Laura, but I haven't the least desire to steal you. As for my being a sexy toad . . . ' He shrugged. 'I've been called worse things.'

'I don't doubt it. Your reputation as a heartbreaker is well known.'

For a moment she thought she'd actually dented his maddening self-assurance, because his face seemed to close up and turn flat. But all he said was, 'Is that so? And I thought I'd been so careful with my hearts.'

'I wouldn't know,' said Laura. She tried to stand up, but found his fingers were still tangled in her hair. 'Do you *mind*?' she asked pointedly.

'Yes, as a matter of fact I do,' he replied, bunching the hair up behind her head. But he let her go.

As she walked toward the door, he added in a deep, steady voice she hadn't heard him use before, 'Be careful, Laura. For you, I think marriage is for keeps. Don't make a mistake you'll regret for the rest of your life.'

Laura hesitated, and then went on walking. 'Why should you care?' she scoffed.

She didn't wait for his answer.

That night it took her a long time to fall asleep. She kept remembering Rodney's face changing colours like a confused traffic light, and Adam's voice warning her to be careful because marriage was for keeps. He was right about that. For her, marriage would indeed be for keeps. She thought again of her mother, and of her friend, Tracy, and the hurt that broken promises could wreak. Surely Rodney deserved better than that, even though he wasn't the type to jump off a bridge. But — was it fair to marry him when, as Adam had so graphically proved, she didn't love him?

Adam. Why had he done it? Why had

he deliberately set her body on fire when he quite openly admitted he didn't want her for himself? He must have meant it too, because, unlike her, he had seemed totally unaffected by the skirmish on the loveseat.

'He did it because he's a toad,' she muttered, as she at last began to drift off to sleep. 'A toad and a pirate and a devil.' And how she was going to get through another month of him was a problem she would face in the morning.

To her relief, Adam didn't appear for breakfast. When she asked where he was, Lancelot grunted and said he supposed he'd gone to pick up his car.

Oh, so the man came with a car. No doubt some flashy sports job, thought Laura with a contemptuous sniff. But it was time to leave for work. The day would go much better if she could manage to put both Adam and Rodney out of her mind.

This turned out to be much easier than expected, mostly because of the odd mood Charlene seemed to be in.

Her friend wouldn't meet her eyes when Laura bid her a casual good morning, and she kept trying to give customers donuts when they asked for bread, and almond cookies when they wanted apple squares or tarts. When Laura asked if there was some reason her mind wasn't on the job, Charlene muttered that she, Laura, ought to know. Laura didn't know, and she was left feeling puzzled and confused. But at least it kept her thoughts off Adam and Rodney.

It was a pensive Laura who ploughed her way up the Allan driveway that evening. Lost in her own thoughts, she didn't notice the battered blue car of indeterminate breed until she had walked smack into the back of it and scraped her shin on the bumper.

'Ouch,' she said, hefting her bag on her shoulder and glaring at the rusty strip of chrome. 'Who — what the hell . . . ?'

'Such unladylike language,' drawled a voice from the other side of the car.

97

Laura raised her head, and was at once transfixed by the sight of an impressive male backside protruding enticingly from under the hood. She hadn't seen it from precisely that angle before, but she had no doubt about whose body it belonged to.

'Is this rustbucket yours?' she asked grumpily, glancing down at the bruise on her leg.

The backside disappeared and straightened into a ragged black T-shirt covering a broad and well-muscled chest.

'It is. And please don't call her names. This, my girl, is a Belvedere. I'm restoring her.'

'Belvedere?' said Laura faintly.

Adam nodded and gave the roof of the car a proprietorial pat. 'My trusty transportation.'

'You call this rustheap transportation? It's an eyesore. And it's blocking the driveway.'

Adam's eyes glittered. 'We're talking about a collector's item, blue-eyes. And I told you not to insult her.'

'Oh, for heaven's sake.' Laura had been feeling irritable even before she got home. Now her leg was hurting, and Adam was looking at her as if he actually thought he had a *right* to tell her what to do. 'I'll call her whatever I please. She's hardly a gold-plated Cadillac.'

'No, that's at home in Vancouver. My sister's driving it at the moment. Tell me, if I *had* introduced you to the Cadillac, would you be behaving with better grace?'

The cool, patronizing edge to his voice inflamed Laura's normally serene temper even more. 'Probably,' she snapped. 'At least we wouldn't look like a junkyard.'

Adam's eyes narrowed. 'Well, well,' he murmured. 'So little Miss Allan likes to keep up appearances for the neighbors. And a Cadillac would impress them nicely. Is that it?'

The bump on Laura's leg began to throb. She didn't care at all about impressing the neighbors, and on top of everything else the unfair accusation was too much.

'No,' she shouted, forgetting that she didn't approve of shouting. 'That is not it. But you have no right to come barging in here with your rusty rattletrap and — ' She stopped abruptly. There was a retaliatory look about Adam that she didn't like, and suddenly she saw herself as he must see her. A near hysterical female carrying on like a spoiled duchess about something as unimportant as the appearance of his car. Not that it was really the car that was making her behave so untypically. But he couldn't know that. Or could he? she wondered wildly, as Adam wiped his hands on a rag and took a slow and purposeful step toward her.

'I see the blue-eyed witch has a temper,' he drawled. 'Maybe it's time I did something to fix that.'

Laura put a steadying hand on the Belvedere. 'Stay away from me,' she said quickly, not trusting that narrow-eyed look. 'You can't — '

'Oh, but I can.' Before she had a chance to back away, strong arms had closed about her waist. A second later, firm lips descended on her mouth, cutting off whatever she'd meant to say. Not that it mattered. As the world around her slid into oblivion, and a warm, wonderful weakness invaded her body, she no longer knew or cared what she'd meant to say. All she cared about was the feel of Adam's hard frame as she strained against him, and the invading sweetness of a kiss like no other kiss she had ever known.

He ended it too soon, leaving her flushed, heated and out of breath, while he draped himself against the Belvedere and smiled with a cynical satisfaction. Laura, still shaking with a half-formed longing, was left wondering if he'd felt anything at all.

'Why did you do that?' she whispered, gripping the strap of her shoulder-bag as if it were some sort of lifeline.

'To sweeten you up, of course.

Besides, I discovered I wanted to, and you gave me an excuse. So now . . . '
He stopped suddenly and glanced at the road behind her. When Laura turned to see what he was looking at, she realized that a solid gray Volvo had pulled to a stop at the curb. She gasped, gave a groan of despair.

Behind her Adam murmured drily, 'Hmm. If I'm not mistaken, something has put our up-and-coming accountant out of sorts.'

4

Laura stared at Rodney's pinched face framed in the window of his car. She didn't believe this. Adam had only been in town a few days, yet she felt as if she had played this scene over and over. First Adam would precipitate some crisis, and immediately afterwards, and at the most awkward moment possible, Rodney would turn up to make things worse. Then Adam would laugh.

She took a deep, steadying breath and squared her shoulders. It was not going to happen this time. This time things would be different.

They were.

Rodney's voice, brittle as ice, clipped through the soft evening air. 'I see I was wrong, Laura. You had no trouble making up your mind.'

Laura, distraught and remorseful, put

her hands up to cover her face. When she lowered them, Rodney was revving up the engine of the Volvo.

'No,' she cried, springing to life and hurling herself down the driveway. 'No, Rodney, wait.'

He waited, but didn't turn off the engine.

Laura caught hold of the window-frame. 'Rodney, please, I'm sorry, I never meant — '

'I realize that, Laura,' he said stiffly. 'It's entirely obvious that you haven't the backbone to stand up to Svengali over there.'

Laura bit back a heated retort. If it made Rodney feel better to blame everything on her — well, what did it matter? Besides, he was more than half right. Adam did have a debilitating effect on her willpower.

'Of course,' Rodney went on, 'if you have now seen the error of your ways . . . ' He paused to clear his throat. 'Naturally I can't overlook — '

Laura didn't hear any more. Vaguely,

the words 'disgraceful', 'improper', and 'unbecoming' penetrated the dizziness in her brain. But none of it made any difference. Because suddenly, she knew with stunning certainty that no matter what Rodney said or did, she couldn't marry him. Fondness and promises were not strong enough foundations for a marriage. Why she hadn't seen it before was something she would figure out later. But at least she had seen it in time.

'Rodney.' She interrupted him in mid-flow. 'Rodney, I can't marry you. And I don't think you really want to marry me.'

Rodney's nose seemed to grow longer. 'I believe I'm the better judge of that,' he said huffily.

'No.' She shook her head. 'No, you're not. Rodney, you've never even tried to make love to me — '

His neck grew longer too. 'In view of your age and inexperience I felt excessive physical contact would be inappropriate.' He spoke with such lofty condescension that Laura had to stop herself from reaching out to tweak his nose. She wondered if what he really meant was that he had never felt any great desire. For her, anyway. That, at least, would explain his reaction to her kiss.

'Rodney,' she said, 'why on earth did you ask me to marry you?'

He shrugged. 'You were young and sweet and anxious to oblige. I thought I could turn you into the kind of wife who would suit me.'

'Well, it seems you couldn't.' Laura stared down at the ring on her finger. She swallowed, as the sun cast a bright diamond flash against the car frame. 'Rodney, I thought you loved me.'

Rodney looked honestly surprised. 'I was fond of you,' he said, as if he couldn't believe any right-thinking woman would ask for more.

Laura nodded. Slowly she drew the ring from her finger. To her confusion, there were tears in her eyes. She had been wearing it for almost three years.

'I hope you'll be happy,' she whispered, handing him the diamond.

'Why shouldn't I be?' he replied brusquely, taking the ring from her and slipping it into his breast pocket.

Laura stared at him dumbly, trying to find the right words to express her regret. But before she could speak, Rodney had shifted into gear and driven off without looking back.

He hadn't even tried to touch her, she realized as she watched him go. And they hadn't exchanged so much as a parting kiss.

For a few seconds she gazed after him, stunned, hurt and unable to form a single coherent thought. When she finally turned round, meaning to head for the comforting cocoon of her bedroom, she found herself slap up against Adam's chest. He was standing right behind her with his hands hanging loosely at his sides, and at once his arms came up and wrapped around her shoulders.

'Let me go,' she cried, beginning to

struggle. 'Don't you know this is all because of you?'

'Not all,' he said soothingly. 'Although I admit I may have helped it along.'

'Helped it . . . ' She fought to hang on to her breath. 'Don't you care at all that you've broken two people's hearts?'

'Don't be ridiculous.' Adam's voice was no longer soothing. 'You know as well as I do that Fosdyke's heart is by no means broken. And you, if I'm not mistaken, are much relieved.'

'Relieved! I am not remotely . . . ' She stopped. His eyes were black pinpoints of light, piercing right through her lie — and she knew she couldn't fool herself again. She was reeling from the feel of his lean body against her own, from the scent of him and from the lure of his full lips, barely parted and seductively close to her mouth. How could she possibly pretend she loved Rodney, when she felt like flinging her arms around Adam and dancing a jig with him to celebrate her freedom? Oh, she still felt remorse, and a wistful regret for lost dreams, but it was as if a great burden had been lifted from her heart.

Adam was right. She was greatly relieved. But how could she admit that to this footloose buccaneer who was reputed to collect women like butter-flies? Not that he meant to collect *her*, she remembered with a pang of inexcusable disappointment.

'Please let me go,' she repeated, refusing to give in to the sensuous heaviness of limbs which longed to stay locked with his forever.

She half expected him to argue, but instead he released her at once.

When she met his eyes, she was surprised to see a flicker of what might have been compassion. But instead of waiting to find out, she dodged around him and ran down the driveway to the house.

Adam made no attempt to follow.

As Laura pushed open the front door and stumbled into the hall, she heard her father's voice booming something sepulchral about 'Conquering Kings'. He was accompanied by a squealing chorus from Ethan's room.

She groaned again and hurried up the stairs to her bedroom, where she slumped down at her desk and fixed blank eyes on the tendrils of ivy doing a gentle cotillion round her window. Had Rodney truly been indifferent to the breaking of their engagement? And had she *never* truly loved him as she thought she had? They had been engaged for so long that surely neither of them ought to feel relief. It wasn't right. A promise was a promise. Just as kissing Adam had been an act of betrayal.

She *couldn't* have inherited her mother's wanton genes. Could she? She dropped her head on to her hands.

All her life she had vowed she would never follow in her dead mother's foot-steps. Because even as a child she had somehow known that Leah Ashton's death wasn't entirely an accident, that her father's grief was for the loss of his wife's love as well as her life. Lancelot had always been loyal, though. He hadn't looked at another woman in all these years, until Primrose de Vere came along. Laura had learned of her mother's infidelity from other people. Not from the father who had kept alive for his children the memory of a loving and devoted mother.

Laura pulled a lock of hair through her fingers. If only she could have been as loyal to Rodney as her father had been to his Leah. It didn't matter that Rodney hadn't loved her. Loyalty and good faith should have stopped her from responding with such abandon to Adam.

She stared at the bright summer green of the cherry tree that grew taller every year outside her window. How *could* she have behaved so like her mother?

'Because of Adam Veryan,' she answered her own question out loud.

A branch of the cherry tree tapped against the glass. Laura sighed. All right, so she and Rodney had never been made for each other. But Adam had had no right to interfere with her life. Not when he didn't even want her for himself.

'Laura Allan! What are you thinking of? You don't want that arrogant, self-satisfied toad any more than he wants you.'

When her only answer was a faint rustling of leaves outside the window, she stood up, walked over to the bed, and flung herself down on the nearest pillow — which turned out to be a silver-grey cat. She sat up again quickly. 'Sorry, Silky,' she muttered, shifting to the other pillow and discovering it was occupied by Silky's twin brother, Silver. Silver fixed her with an unblinking, 'No Trespassing' eye.

Laura shook her head and sat up, feeling suddenly stifled. She needed air, and a quiet place to sort out her thoughts.

It was cooler outside in the garden, but because her mind had gone comfortingly numb, she didn't see the brown and white object streaking across the lawn until her legs were swept from under her by what appeared to be a jet-propelled rug. She struggled to her knees, and discovered that, as usual, the rug was Pal in pursuit of next door's cat. A moment later the pursuer became the pursued as the cat turned on its tormentor and chased Pal back across the lawn.

Laura rolled out of the flight path and came to rest under a rhododendron bush. When all seemed calm again, she picked herself up resignedly and began to brush dust off her clothes.

'I've heard of a roll in the hay,' Adam murmured from somewhere above her. 'But a roll in the rhododendrons . . . ?'

'Oh, shut up.' She was in no mood for banter, especially from him.

He caught her arm. 'Don't you tell me to shut up,' he said, quite pleasantly but in a voice that meant business. 'I won't put up with it, you know.'

'Oh? And how do you propose to

stop me?' She tried, unsuccessfully, to shake him off.

He put his head on one side and half lowered his sleepy-looking eyelids. 'There are several alternatives, I suppose.'

Suddenly Laura sensed danger in the air, and stepped away from him.

At once Adam's expression changed, became colder, and he shook his head. 'No,' he said. 'I may be an opportunist, but I draw the line at hitting a man when he's down. Or, in this case, kissing a woman less than an hour after she's broken off her engagement.'

'It didn't bother you five minutes *before* I broke it off,' she pointed out, acutely conscious that he still had her arm firmly in his grip.

'True. But at that stage I wasn't sure you'd seen the light.'

'Light? What light?'

'The one that showed you Fosdyke in his true colours,' he explained patiently.

'But . . . ' Laura scowled, and tried once again to remove her arm. 'But what difference does that make? Why should you care if I see Rodney in purple and gold stripes with pink trim?'

Adam brushed a hand across his mouth. 'Irresistible,' he murmured. 'And I shouldn't mind at all.'

'That's not an answer,' she snapped.

'You want an answer? All right, you can call my interest sheer quixotery if you like.'

'I don't like. I see nothing quixotic about orchestrating the end of an engagement.'

'No, I suppose you wouldn't.' His voice was flat, a little bored.

'Adam . . . ' Laura tried to sound calm, but it was difficult when she could feel the heat coming off his body, and the pressure of his fingers on her arm. 'Adam, why were you so anxious to mess up my life?'

'You've got it backwards, blue-eyes. I wanted to stop *you* messing it up.'

Laura curled her fists into her palms. 'If, by that, you mean you wanted to stop me marrying Rodney — '

'Not at first. Although your father had hopes.'

'But why? *Why* should you care?' Waiting for his answer, she discovered her heart was beating faster than it should.

After studying her face for a moment, Adam shrugged and said offhandedly, 'It's not so much that I care, as that I have seen my sister, who is normally an intelligent woman, marry the wrong man once too often. I didn't want to see you make the same mistake.'

'I see,' Laura replied frigidly. 'As you said, pure quixotery on your part.'

'What else?' He curved his hand round the back of her neck. When she shivered, he laughed softly.

Laura opened her mouth to say, 'Sheer interfering, overbearing bossiness.' But somehow the words never got out, because Adam was looking down at her with a curious, half startled glitter in his eyes, as if he had seen something unexpected that didn't please him. His free hand was brushing abstractedly over her rear. And suddenly her head was spinning, her blood was singing and his lips were only inches away.

With a moan that was part distress and part pure physical need, she threw her arms around his waist and arched her body into his.

For a second she dreamed she felt him respond. But then, incredibly, he had taken her wrists and was holding her firmly away.

'I'm flattered,' he said. 'But no. The idea was to prevent mistakes, not make them.'

'Oh!' Laura caught her breath and willed herself not to drop her eyes. She would *not* let him see her hurt and shame. But when she met his gaze she didn't see the mockery she expected. Adam was frowning, his skin was unusually dark, and he seemed angry, as if he'd been confronted with a surprise he didn't like.

For no reason, Laura felt her spirits lighten. 'You're right of course,' she said airily. 'You certainly are a mistake.'

'Hm.' Adam put his fingers under her chin and tilted it up quite roughly. 'We still haven't cured that tongue of yours, have we? A task I'll look forward to with pleasure.'

'Toad.' Seeing his eyebrows sweep threateningly upwards, Laura swallowed hard and glared.

He ignored the glare and cast a disparaging glance over her dusty clothing. 'Stop scowling at me,' he ordered. 'And go and get changed. I'm taking you out for a post-engagement dinner.'

Laura felt the last remnant of her control snap like a branch in the wind. Up until this moment she'd been partly numb, helpless in the grip of bodily urges which kept scrambling the danger signals she would normally have had no trouble receiving. But Adam's careless reference to the break-up of her long-term engagement — a break-up of which he had been the cause — brought all her resentment seething to the surface.

'No,' she said, her body stiff with fury and her voice shaking. 'No, we are not going to dinner. Half an hour ago I was still engaged to Rodney.' She broke off to dash the back of her hand across cheeks which, inexplicably, seemed to be wet. 'And now, because of your interfering arrogance, it's all over. What gives you the right to meddle with my life, you overbearing — ?'

'Hey.' Adam laid a heavy hand on her shoulder. 'Cut it out, blue-eyes. Believe me, I understand that your Rodney had become something of a habit, but don't call me names for shaking you out of your rut. You know damn well you didn't love him — any more than he loved you.'

'You still had no right. And I gave him my word — '

'Which he, very sensibly, gave back. Laura, you two suited each other about as well as a turkey would match up with a canary — '

'Rodney is not a turkey.'

'And I didn't say you were any

canary,' he pointed out, rubbing a handkerchief across her damp cheeks. 'Not if your father's voice is anything to go by. Now — let's not waste any more tears. You can stop pretending you feel any real regrets, and get changed into something less dusty. Then we're going out.' He didn't wait for her reply, but came round behind her, put a hand in the small of her back, and began to propel her firmly toward the house.

'Oh, no, we're not,' said Laura, more angry than ever — partly because he was right about her lack of regret, and partly because she hadn't meant to cry. She hated him seeing the tears that she couldn't explain even to herself.

'Oh, yes, we are.' Adam was amiably confident.

'We're not. Besides, I have to make supper for Dad and Ethan.'

'No, you don't. I've arranged to have Chinese sent in.'

'They don't like — '

'Yes, they do. They chose it.'

Laura tried to stop dead, but found

she was still being pushed toward the house. 'What did you say? They can't have. And *you* can't have known that Rodney and I would — would . . . '

'Sever all ties? No, but I still meant to take you to dinner. Your father thought an evening away from Fosdyke would do you good.'

This time she succeeded in swinging round — only to find herself backed up against the door with his hands on either side of her head. She gazed into dark, determined eyes and shivered suddenly — not, she realized, with fear, but with anticipation. The knowledge made her choke back a gasp.

'How — how did you expect to achieve that?' she asked, not bothering to hide her disbelief. 'By kidnapping me? Or did you imagine I'd find your company irresistible?'

'Kidnapping if necessary. But I suppose I'd prefer it if you found me irresistible. Does that answer your question?' He smiled at her, that white, implacable smile that showed his teeth.

'I guess it does,' Laura was almost, but not quite, too exhausted to argue any more. 'Would you let me go, please? I have no intention of being kidnapped, Adam, and it may surprise you to know I'm very good at resisting.'

His eyebrows shot up. 'You are? Does that mean our friend Fosdyke was even less persuasive than I thought?'

'It means whatever you want it to mean,' said Laura tiredly. 'I said let me go.'

'Only if you promise to stop arguing and do what you're told.'

'And if I don't?' she asked, with a sweetness that was meant to be deceptive.

'There are other options.' He moved one hand to the nape of her neck and began to stroke it.

Laura twisted her head, and he moved his fingers under the collar of her blouse.

'Why do you want me to go out with you?' She leaned her head back, pretending she didn't notice what he was doing, and hoping he would go on doing it.

'Do you have a better idea?'

Yes, just at this moment she did. But it wasn't the sort of idea she was in the habit of discussing with men she hardly knew. Or men she knew very well, for that matter. 'Yes. Well, no, not really . . . '

His thumb began massaging the area just below her left ear. Laura felt a familiar heat sear down the middle of her back, and at the same moment she heard Ethan's distinctive whistle advancing up the street. It was accompanied by a noise that resembled a bagpipe trying to imitate a bugle.

And right there, backed up against the door, her resistance crumbled as if it had never existed. She couldn't fight Adam any longer; she was too drained. And she wasn't up to an evening with the bagpipe. Not tonight, when her whole world had been turned upside down and shaken so severely that her head felt like the inside of a paint mixer.

'All right,' she said dully. 'I'll have dinner with you. You win.'

'I usually do,' he murmured drily. 'But with more enthusiasm on the part of the prize.'

'I'm the prize?' Laura leaned her head against the door and stared at a puffball cloud hanging above the fir trees. 'I didn't think prizes were awarded for coercion.'

'Is that what you call it?' For a moment something dark and baffled shimmered in Adam's eyes. But almost at once it was replaced by the familiar black glitter.

'What would *you* call it?' she asked wearily.

'Perseverance in the face of opposition. A refusal to give up at the first setback.'

'Why bother?' asked Laura. 'And breaking up someone's engagement goes a lot further than mere perseverance.'

At that she felt Adam's fingers tangle in her hair. 'We've been over that already,' he said in a voice that grated over her frayed nerve-ends like sand-paper. 'But if you can look me in the eye and tell me you love Rodney Fosdyke, I'll move heaven and earth to convince him to take you back.'

Laura looked into his eyes. They were hard, unrelenting, with no trace of the mockery she was used to, and she knew that he meant every word. Without mercy, he was going straight for the jugular, forcing her to abandon the pretences she had hidden behind for so long. The pretences she had needed in order to avoid the unpalatable truth that she and Rodney were unsuited in every way.

'I — I'm very fond of Rodney,' she hedged.

'Laura?' His black gaze stripped away the prevarication, and her eyes dropped to the well-worn sandals on his feet.

'No. I don't love him,' she admitted. 'But I did owe him my loyalty and good faith.'

'Fine. If you say so.' He lifted her

chin and gave her a smile that made him look several shades less dangerous and twice as sexy. 'Me you owe the pleasure of your company.'

'Pleasure? I wouldn't count on it.' She returned his smile, making an effort to look as though his careless charisma left her unaffected. Then she turned to go into the house.

But as Adam muttered something she didn't catch and gave her a casual pat on the thigh that made her gasp, she heard a youthful voice exclaim gleefully, 'Holy Toledo. Laura, don't tell me you've dumped Rodney at last. Are you going to kiss Adam instead?'

'She already has. She's not going to do it again just at present. And any more remarks like that from you, young man, and you may wish you'd kept your mouth zipped.' Adam spoke in a friendly, perfectly even tone that caused Ethan to mumble a hasty 'sorry'.

'No problem,' replied Adam, urging Laura ahead of him.

She made straight for the stairs,

anxious to be alone for a while, but when she reached the landing she heard a strange sound coming from behind her. It took her a few seconds to realize it was only Howard, snuggled into Ethan's arms, and apparently doing his best impersonation of a beginner's class in basic violin.

Laura shuddered. Yes, on the whole, and in spite of all that had happened she was glad she wouldn't be spending the evening at home. On the other hand, considering the alternative was Adam . . . She groaned aloud. Why on earth had she agreed to go out with him? His company only confused her, made her behave in ways she had never even thought of before. How *could* she have kissed him? And why did he insist on taking her to dinner now that he had successfully accomplished what he set out to do?

She wandered over to her wardrobe. Perhaps it was just his idea of being kind. No. More likely his idea of getting his own way, she decided, tugging a hanger viciously off the rail. He and her father had planned Operation Eliminate Rodney, and, now that they had succeeded, saw no reason to change the evening's agenda.

She frowned, and began to pull on her best cream silk dress with the draped neckline and full wraparound skirt.

★   ★   ★

The restaurant Adam had chosen was some miles out of town in a large, gabled house set well back from the highway at the end of a long, tree-lined avenue. Perched on the cliffs above the ocean, it commanded a breath-taking view of misty islands and soft, mauve-tinted ocean. Well-manicured lawns, a summerhouse and colourful rosebeds gave it the air of a transplanted English country mansion.

'Oh,' cried Laura, delighted out of her weariness and resentment. 'It's beautiful. I'd heard of the Sanctuary, of course, but I've never been here.'

'No? Surely you're not trying to tell me that Fosdyke's taste ran more to fish 'n' chips?'

'Rodney's taste ran more to his mother's cooking. Or mine in a pinch. We didn't eat out often.'

'I told you you'd had a lucky escape.'

Laura didn't answer. This morning she'd been engaged to Rodney. She wasn't about to start running him down in the evening. But in her heart she knew Adam was right.

The restaurant was in keeping with the exterior of the house, all dark mahogany tables, high-backed chairs and pictures of horses and dogs on ivory-papered walls.

They were shown at once to a quiet table overlooking the water.

Laura was half afraid Adam would have the bad taste to order champagne to celebrate the end of her engagement. But he didn't, settling instead on a good Chardonnay to complement the poached salmon they both ordered.

At first they made desultory small talk about the view, and the antics of Adam's nieces and nephews, of whom he seemed fond in a non-committal way. Laura discovered that he could be a relaxing and amusing companion when he chose to keep his buccaneer instincts in check, so she wasn't prepared for the change in atmosphere that came a few moments after the waiter brought the dessert.

'Have you made up your mind yet?' Adam asked suddenly, in a voice that for some reason made her jump. 'About what college you mean to attend?'

Laura swallowed a sinfully fattening mouthful of fruit torte. 'College? I — no. Not yet. I haven't thought — '

'Then start thinking. Your father wants you to go.'

Oh. So that was what this was all about. Laura laid down her fork, wondering why she suddenly felt betrayed. 'I know he does,' she said. 'And I suppose he enlisted your help to get Rodney out of the picture. Is this dinner just your way of finishing off the job, clearing up loose ends, so to speak? Loose ends like college.'

Adam frowned. 'What are you suggesting?'

'That you're only carrying out Dad's orders. Was that why you kissed me?'

For just an instant his eyes blazed blue-black fire. Then they turned blank. 'If memory serves, a few hours ago *you* kissed me. And I've done a lot of things I didn't want to do in my time, but kissing a woman is not one of them.'

'Oh.' Laura dropped her gaze to a large and luscious-looking black cherry. She wasn't sure what to answer to that, but her pulse seemed to be beating abnormally fast. 'Of course I mean to go to college,' she said quickly, returning to a less risky topic. 'I always intended to get my degree.'

'When?'

'Well, Rodney wanted me at home — '

'And you caved in to that kind of old-fashioned chauvinism? Surely if you're old enough to marry, you ought to be old enough to make your own decisions.'

Laura clutched the edge of the table, willing herself not to throw her fruit torte at his head. Not that it wouldn't serve him right.

'No, I did not cave in,' she snapped, leaning across the table and thrusting out her jaw. 'I *compromised* by agreeing to go later. Just because *you've* lived a life filled with excitement and adventure, with the freedom to do as you please, it doesn't mean the rest of the world doesn't have responsibilities — '

Adam interrupted her. 'Excitement and adventure? I suppose that's true, if your idea of excitement is endless waiting about for something to happen, followed by the prospect of imminent death.' He glowered down at the fist he was pressing against the snow-white tablecloth. 'I've seen men go mad with the waiting.'

His eyes were bleak now, and Laura knew he was remembering horrors she couldn't begin to imagine. To him she was just a dull little country girl who had lived a comparatively easy life, and had no conception of the seriousness of his work. A dull little country girl who had given up her dreams of college to marry a dull country man.

'I didn't mean it that way,' she said, quite calmly now.

'Didn't you?' He smiled cynically, and with an abrupt movement pushed his plate away. 'Tell me something, Laura. Since you obviously entertain the odd fanciful, if inaccurate, notion about life in the world outside of Cinnamon Bay, why did it take you so long to figure out that you had a right to taste it for yourself? Your father tells me you've dreamed of college for years, but that Fosdyke wouldn't even consider it.'

Oh, so now she was slow-thinking as well as dull. Fine college material, that! She stirred her coffee so vigorously that it splashed into the saucer. Of course there was no reason why she should answer his less than flattering question.

But, inexplicably, she wanted him to know, wanted him to understand that loyalty, to her, was more than just a word.

In the end, her answer seemed to form by itself.

'I always knew I had the right,' she replied. 'But by the time I realized Rodney would never approve, I was engaged to him. And in a way I could see his point. It's not unreasonable to want a family while you're young.'

'You'll still be young in three or four years. Too damn young. Why didn't you tell Fosdyke he could wait?'

Laura fixed her gaze on a picture of two golden retrievers gamboling in a field. 'Because I'm a fool, I suppose.'

'That thought had crossed my mind.' Adam took a long swallow of coffee while he watched her over the rim of his cup.

Laura choked back the indignant words that sprang to her lips, because she saw that, once again, he wanted to see how much she could take before being provoked into losing her temper.

'We all make mistakes,' she said. 'But you see, if I'd told Rodney he had to wait, he would have taken it as a permanent rejection. And I didn't want to reject him. I'd made him a promise, and my word is something I value.' She took a deep breath, tried to carry on as if what she was telling him didn't hurt. 'I don't know if anyone told you — if they didn't, they soon will — but my mother was leaving my father when she was killed. It broke his heart. I don't want to be like her.' She spoke jerkily, in a low voice, because the pain of the past was still with her. It tore her apart to talk of those days. But she *had* to make Adam understand. She didn't know why, but she had to.

When he leaned across the table and placed his hand over the fingers she had curled into a fist, for a while at least, she thought she had succeeded.

'You won't be like her,' he said. 'Yes, I heard about your mother. Primrose de Vere told me.' Laura said nothing, and after a moment he went on in a different, more abrasive tone, 'It's over, Laura. Time to move on.'

Laura pulled her hand from under his and wrapped her napkin around it on her lap. 'Maybe it is. But I cared about Rodney. I suppose, in a way, I always will.'

Adam's mouth turned down. 'Then either you're out of your mind, or he's a better man than I thought.'

'Yes. I expect he is.' Laura had had all the interference from Adam she meant to take. 'He was certainly gentleman enough to come to the rescue of a naïve and timid teenager when she needed him.'

'You?' Adam's eyebrows slanted upward. 'Inexperienced and unsophisticated, perhaps. But naïve and timid?'

Was he laughing at her? He usually was. 'I was all that and more when I met Rodney,' replied Laura, tossing her head. She wasn't sure why she was bothering to explain, but something in Adam's eyes made her go on.

'It was the summer after graduation, and I'd just started working at the bakery. My friend Tracy gave a party for her boyfriend's birthday. I was very shy and nobody asked me to dance, so I went out to sit in the garden. I should have known better, because Larry the Lecher — that's Larry Lovejoy — was out there waiting to pounce.'

'Larry the Lecher?' Adam lifted an eyebrow.

'He's Cinnamon Bay's Peeping Tom. Only sometimes he doesn't stop at peeping.'

'Is there any point in my asking why he isn't locked up?'

'I think he was a couple of times. But he's more of a nuisance than a danger.'

'Sure. Until some unfortunate woman ends up losing more than she bargained for.'

He sounded so disgusted that Laura found herself leaping to Larry's defence. 'No, really, he's not that bad. It's just that he thinks he's God's gift to women.'

'Then if he's so damned harmless,

how come our estimable accountant got to play knight in shining armour?'

Laura sighed. Adam was obviously in no mood to make allowances for the town's self-appointed Romeo. But the truth was, on that long-ago evening, Larry had put a clammy hand where it had no business, and mumbled that her sweet mouth was like a warm tomato ripe for tasting. Somehow she didn't feel like telling Adam that.

'Larry was trying to kiss me,' she said briefly. 'He wouldn't leave me alone. Until Rodney appeared out of the blue and threatened to hit him. Larry left then, at once, and Rodney stayed behind to calm me down. He was very kind. Brotherly, in a way. I'd seen him around town before, of course, but he'd never paid me any attention. After that evening, he did.'

At the time, Laura remembered, she had assumed Rodney was merely being chivalrous, but a few days later he had called to ask her out. It was a month after that before he kissed her, a chaste kiss that left her feeling dissatisfied. Vaguely, she had been aware that, for Rodney, at least part of her attraction was her innocence, and her willingness to fall in with his plans. For her part she continued to see him as her personal knight-errant — although it was hard to think of Larry as a true villain. She wasn't sure just when Rodney's sword had begun to seem a bit tarnished, but as she grew older, and became aware of bodily needs that hadn't been there before, it did occur to her that his polite respect for her virtue was unusual. She also began to wonder about his not infrequent trips to the Mainland.

A waiter came by to refill their coffee-cups, and Laura was brought back to the subdued elegance of the Sanctuary by the sound of Adam's disbelieving laugh. 'Are you trying to tell me you let yourself become attached to our friend Fosdyke merely because he offered to punch some bastard's nose?'

'No, I — '

'Because if that's the case I'll be happy to punch noses in your honour. Just line them up. Fosdyke will do nicely for a start.'

'Oh, do stop being ridiculous.' Laura didn't know whether she wanted to laugh or cry.

'Ridiculous?' Adam leaned forward and rested his forearms on the table. He was smiling his night and day smile. 'For your information, I'm good at handling noses. And you do kiss rather promisingly, Miss Allan.'

5

Laura felt a pulse beat crazily just below her right eye, and she put up a hand to conceal it. 'What do you mean?' she asked stiffly.

Adam picked up his cup and swallowed the remainder of his coffee in one gulp. 'It shouldn't be hard to figure out.'

'Are you saying you've changed your mind about kissing people who have just broken off their engagements?' Laura cast a wary eye on the large hands curved around the cup.

'Maybe I am.' His reply was curt, his eyes hooded, and Laura was left feeling breathless and vaguely alarmed. He didn't seem to be teasing any more.

'But — you're not interested in me. You said so.'

'So I did.' He sat back. 'You, on the other hand, have indicated that you're not entirely immune to my . . . ' He paused, strummed his fingers on the table. 'Shall we say charms?'

Laura stared at him, lounging back in his chair looking powerful and confident in a black suit. There was a hard little smile on his lips, and she had a feeling that, interested or not, at this moment he didn't like her very much. Or else that he did, and wondered why.

'What charms?' she scoffed — but without conviction. 'And it was only a kiss. That's hardly a proposal of marriage.'

'Marriage?' he repeated, and for a moment Laura thought she had thrown him off balance. 'No, I didn't suppose you'd go that far. But there are some stimulating possibilities that fall quite a way short of the altar.' His mouth curved suggestively, and his sexy drawl seemed to wrap around her body like heated silk. She withdrew her gaze from the taunting invitation in his eyes, and it fell on the muscular chest so ineffectively concealed by his shirt.

142

Laura swallowed, and moistened her lips. 'Adam — ' She squared her shoulders to convince herself she meant what she was saying. 'Adam, I don't care for egotistical men who upset other people's lives for no reason. So you needn't harbour any illusions that I'm about to tumble into your bed.'

His smile narrowed, and he signalled the waiter for more coffee. 'I haven't upset anyone's life,' he told her bluntly. 'But if I had it would have been for a reason. As for illusions — I lost mine a long time ago. The inevitable result of a close acquaintance with humanity's preoccupation with war. Watching men kill each other, often on the most trivial of pretexts, doesn't exactly encourage illusion, Laura.'

No, it wouldn't, she thought, studying the lines fanning out around those eyes that had seen too much, and noting the sudden flattening of his mouth. But if Adam saw things as clearly as he seemed to think he did, then why . . . ?

'If that's true, why are you wasting your time — what's that English expression? Chatting me up?' she demanded, putting her thoughts into words.

'I never waste my time. And chatting isn't what I have in mind.'

'No,' said Laura. 'Bed is.'

'Hole in one,' agreed Adam, putting down his cup. 'Bed for you, young lady. Immediately and alone. Drink up, I'm taking you home.'

'Why?' she scoffed. 'Because I won't give you what you want?'

'No. Because it's getting late and you look tired. Oh, and by the way, I have an idea you *would* give me what I want. If I wanted it. Which, at the moment, I don't.'

Laura set her cup down with a clatter. 'I don't know what makes you think that,' she said frigidly. 'I was going to marry Rodney, and we never . . . ' She broke off when she saw the sudden startled glitter in Adam's eye.

'How many years did you say you

were engaged to him?' he asked.

'Almost three.'

'And you never — '

'No. Never.' Laura lifted her chin, wondering why she felt foolish about something she ought to be proud of. She could feel two embarrassed spots of colour scorching her cheekbones.

'Are you telling me the truth?' Adam leaned across the table, his expression sharp with disbelief.

'Of course. Why would I lie? Not that it's any of your business,' she added belatedly.

When all he said was, 'Well, I'm damned,' Laura rose to her feet and asked coldly,

'Does that make me some kind of freak?'

Adam rose too. 'No. It makes your Rodney some kind of fool, but . . . ' He came round the table and, in front of all the other diners, took her face in his hands and dropped a featherlight kiss on her lips. 'But I'm glad,' he finished.

'Why? It has nothing to do with you.'

Laura felt her skin tingle as he tucked her wrap around her shoulders and steered her through a door leading out into the garden. 'Where are we going?' she asked. 'This isn't the way back to your beloved Belvedere.'

'No. I changed my mind. We're going for a walk among the roses. Tell me . . . ' He paused for a moment. 'Why did your Rodney put up with it?'

'Put up with what?'

'Your militant virginity.' Abruptly he spun her round to face him, and she saw the last rays of the sun touch his eyes, turning them into black, dangerous caverns.

Laura gulped and felt her mouth go dry, as a wave of something that was part fury and part desire swept over her and left her limp and gasping. But not too limp to raise her hand.

He caught it before it found its mark. 'No,' he said. 'I have a habit of hitting back when I'm attacked. And as I've been taught that it's unchivalrous to hit a woman, I'm afraid I can't allow you to put temptation in my path.'

'Unchivalrous!' scoffed Laura. 'Do you call it chivalrous to make uncalled for remarks about my — my — ?'

'Virginity?' Adam suggested helpfully. 'No, I suppose it wasn't entirely tactful. I apologize. You took me by surprise, that's all.'

'You mean you've never met a woman who wants to save that particular gift for the one special man she will spend her life with?' She could well believe it. His name was mostly linked with high-flying ladies who had no reputations left to lose.

The sun dipped behind the horizon, and a shadow fell across Adam's face. He didn't answer at once, but when he did, his voice had changed, become dry, almost without expression. 'Yes,' he said, turning to stare out over the deep purple ridges of the ocean. 'I did once. But the special man turned out not to be me. My own fault, of course.' He stood silently for a moment, not moving, his big body bulking rigid against the gold of the sky. Then he swung around to face her so quickly that she was taken aback. 'Do you believe in second chances?' he asked.

'Sometimes,' said Laura cautiously, wondering if the woman he'd failed to win had been the ghost he had once called Christine. 'But only for those who deserve them.'

'Which I don't, I suppose?'

'What you deserve,' said Laura, 'is a swift kick in a soft place for being an interfering toad with no conscience.'

Adam shrugged, and she could just see the midnight glitter in his eyes. 'You're probably right,' he agreed. 'In which case I've nothing to lose by proving to you just how right you are.'

She didn't like the sound of that, and Adam looked uncomfortably menacing looming over her in the dusk with the scent of roses heavy on the air. She started to back away.

'And where do you think you're going?' he asked, coming after her and catching her by the shoulder. 'Don't you want to find out just how undeserving I can be?'

'No,' said Laura. 'I don't need proof of what I already know.'

'I think you do. I think you need to have it brought home to you, virtuous maiden, that you too can stray from the straight and narrow. Right now you see me as the wicked villain who ruined your wedding plans — '

'And didn't you?'

'Do we have to go over that again? No, sweet blue-eyes, I didn't. You did. As I'm about to show you.'

'What do you . . . ?' Laura had no chance to finish her sentence, and barely enough time to gasp, before once again Adam had lifted her off her feet and was bearing her in his arms across the lawn. She was still catching her breath when he shouldered open the door of the small square summerhouse she had earlier noticed perched above the cliffs.

Determined not to betray her nervousness, she said drily, 'This is getting altogether monotonous. I'm not a parcel, Adam. Please put me down.'

Adam laughed unsympathetically and laid her carefully on a long padded seat beneath the window. Then he removed her shoes. When he shrugged off his jacket and tossed it against the wall, she remembered his comment about her militant virginity, and began to wonder, with an odd detachment, if she was about to become the traditional sacrifice on the altar of his manhood. Not that the window-seat felt like an altar. In fact it was surprisingly soft . . .

Laura, what are you thinking of? Horrified by her own errant thoughts, she watched Adam remove his tie and pitch it after the jacket. The movement awoke her to the predicament she was in. She sat up quickly and swung her feet to the floor, but in one stride he was beside her and, without quite knowing how it happened, once again she found herself stretched out on the seat. Adam was briskly unbuttoning his shirt.

'What are you doing?' she gulped. 'Don't . . . '

'All right. You do it for me.' He sat down, lifted her hand and placed it on his half-exposed chest.

She felt his skin beneath her fingers, warm and tough and dusted with fine silky hairs. And she could feel the blood pulsing through his veins, echoing the beat of her heart. With a groan she caught at the next button, then the next, and before she knew it Adam's shirt was on the floor.

'You see,' he said, as she ran her palms across his chest in gentle and enthralled exploration.

Laura didn't know what she was supposed to see, but she did know that she was in the grip of emotions and needs she had never come close to before. And Adam was too far away.

She reached up, put her arms around his neck and pulled him down so that she was trapped beneath his body.

He kissed her, lightly at first and then with passion. His hand curved around her breast and she felt the nipple harden and peak as his lips moved oh, so slowly from her mouth to the hollow of her throat. She felt as if every nerve in her body was on fire, and when she moved, crying out for relief, she became conscious that there was a silken barrier between her body and the fulfilment she craved.

Adam wasn't even attempting to take off her dress. As he slid his hand down, moved it agonizingly over her hip and thigh, and then, with gentle torture, back to her breast, she heard herself begging, 'Adam, please, I need, I want — '

'What do you want?' he asked softly.

'You. I want you.' There. She had said it. Now, surely he would help her loose the constraints of her clothing, teach her all the things she longed to know, satisfy this terrible hunger . . .

But he didn't. Instead he sat up, pulled her dress down to her knees, and left her lying there weak with longing, and the beginnings of shame, on the padded seat which all of a sudden felt like hot nails.

'What, why — what are you doing?' she whispered, as she watched him pull on his shirt.

'I'm making myself decent again. As to why — because I'm not in the business of deflowering innocent purveyors of cream buns.' He had his back to her, but she could tell from his rigidly controlled movements that he wasn't as unaffected as he sounded.

'Then why did you start — what you started?' she asked, as passion began to give way to anger.

'Because I wanted to. And because your damn blue-eyed, holier-than-thou sanctimoniousness was beginning to get my goat. And it was the only way I could think of to convince you, finally and forever, that it wasn't I who brought an end to your engagement. Fosdyke couldn't give you what you wanted, and you know it.' He swung round and jerked his tie into place. 'Admit it.'

'Yes. All right, I admit it.' Laura stared at him, so huge in the confines of the summerhouse, so dangerous, and yet so desirable that she would have given anything to lure him back into her arms. 'I admit it. But that doesn't mean I like myself for it. Or you.'

'You don't have to like me. I'm not sure I like myself much either. And if I went too far, I apologize. Although judging from the way you responded, I'm not sure any apology is called for.'

'What do you mean by that?' Laura wanted to hit him, hug him and hide her head, all at the same time.

Adam pulled on his jacket. 'You can hardly plead indifference to me,' he pointed out.

'I can. I am indifferent.'

He laughed, and it wasn't a sound she trusted. 'So you're a liar as well as a fallen angel. You disappoint me.' He held out his hand. 'Come on, Miss Allan, this time I really am taking you home.'

Laura refused to accept the proffered

hand, so with a sigh of exasperation Adam took her by the elbows and hauled her upright. 'Now,' he said, 'are you going to come quietly, or do I have to play caveman again?'

'Why not? It's a role you enjoy, isn't it?' Laura said tartly.

'Mmm. I must say I do on occasion. Is this going to be one of those occasions?'

Laura couldn't see his eyes in the dim light, but she just knew they were gleaming with intent.

'No,' she said. 'I can walk, thank you. If you'll give me time to put on my shoes.'

'Of course.' He rested his shoulders against the wall, and watched while she sat on the window-seat, groped for her shoes, and slipped them on.

After that she made sure she stayed out of his reach as she walked beside him in silence to the car.

Neither of them spoke on the drive back to Cinnamon Bay, and the moment they came to a stop in front of her house Laura was out and hurrying up the driveway. She was almost at the door before Adam turned off the engine and caught up with her.

'Aren't you going to say thank you?' he asked softly.

'For what?'

'Oh — how about for a pleasant evening? And for making you face up to the truth?'

'The truth? I don't even know what the truth is,' exclaimed Laura with unhappy sincerity. 'But I'll thank you for dinner if you like. Goodnight, Adam.'

In the light from the porch she saw his lips twist downward, and had a sense that she had angered him in some way. If she had, he deserved it. All the same, for a moment she hesitated. And, just for a second, she thought he meant to kiss her again. When he didn't, she wasn't sure if she was relieved or disappointed.

Turning away, she put her key in the lock and hurried into the house.

'Goodnight, Laura.' Adam's low drawl followed her all the way up the stairs.

Silver and Silky, ears laid back and tails twitching, were sitting outside Ethan's door looking predatory.

'You two are as bad as Adam,' she muttered, feeling a certain sympathy for Ethan's gerbils. 'Always waiting to pounce.'

She went into her room and shut the door.

Two hours later she was still lying with her arms behind her head gazing at the shadows cast by moonlight on the ceiling.

Adam was right, of course. He had proved to her, quite ruthlessly and with nonchalant brutality, that she didn't love and never had loved Rodney. Yet she must always regrct hcr part in the inevitable break-up. Regret and broken promises and lost dreams. Because she had made those promises not only to Rodney, but to herself.

'What are you doing to me, Adam?'

she whispered, pulling the sheet down to let the night air cool her heated skin. 'Even the thought of you makes my temperature go up. And in just a few days you've changed my life.'

For the better? She wondered, dragging the sheet through her fingers. Yes. Maybe. Marriage to Rodney would have been a disaster. And now, once her father was settled with Primrose, she was free to go to college without dashing the expectations of the man she had once though she loved.

So why was she so restless, so angry with Adam? Why did she want to get up right now, head for the basement, and . . . ?

OK. She knew the answer to that. And it was, of course, the reason she wished Adam Veryan had never erupted into her kitchen, ruined her baked halibut, and made her dream of excitement, adventure, distant lands — and the company of a man who had experienced it all. Adam excited her, aroused her. More than ever after tonight. Quite simply, she wanted him.

But Adam was forever out of bounds.

There was no question of a relationship with a man who would soon be off to risk his life again, a man who had no roots, and who thought nothing of breezing into her world, changing it irrevocably, and then saying callously that he wasn't in the business of deflowering innocent purveyors of cream buns.

For which I should be eternally thankful, she thought bitterly.

Except that she wasn't thankful. She was angry, hurt, and ashamed that she had let him see how easily she succumbed to his appeal. Just as her mother had succumbed to her lover.

An owl hooted in the darkness, and suddenly all the old memories, all the grief and hurt, came surging back — one memory standing out above the others.

Leah Allan in the garden, waving goodbye to them, all bright-eyed and laughing with love — for a man who wasn't her father, only they hadn't known that at the time. She had said she would be away for a few days. But the car her lover was driving had never made it to the ferry, and the two of them had become another grim statistic on the Island Highway.

Since that day, her father had never spoken of her mother in any but the most respectful and loving terms, but Laura had seen the grief and hurt in his eyes, and it hadn't been long before one of her schoolfriends had told her the truth. She hadn't believed it at first, but when Tracy had confirmed the story, and two small boys repeated it to Ethan, she had finally been forced to believe. Shortly after that she had taken over the housekeeping for her father, wanting to make up to him as best she could for all the pain he kept so rigidly to himself.

Laura moved her head restlessly on the pillow. Was she following in her mother's footsteps? Until Adam had come along to shatter her complacency, she had been sure it couldn't happen. No. It still couldn't happen. Never would. If she had made the mistake of marrying Rodney, she would have been faithful to him. In spite of Adam. Wouldn't she?

One of the cats gave a soft meow outside on the landing, and Laura stared glumly up into the blackness, imagining she could see Adam's face in the shadows. He was smiling that incredible, spine-tingling smile.

'Toad,' she muttered. 'You're a heartless, unspeakable toad. If only I didn't want you so much. If only . . . '

She sighed. If only life weren't so confusing. Turning on her side, Laura squeezed her eyes shut and willed herself to fall asleep.

★ ★ ★

'Charlene? What's the matter?' Laura tucked her bag under the counter and looked up to see her friend glancing sideways, as if she didn't want to meet Laura's eyes.

'Nothing.'

'Oh. You seem — Charlene, have I done something wrong?'

'Not that I know of.' Charlene glared murderously at a blueberry muffin.

Laura studied her friend's averted profile. Charlene had been behaving oddly for several weeks now, but today she seemed almost feverishly unsettled. The glitter in her brown eyes was too bright, and her cheeks were too pink. Laura touched her arm. 'It's Rodney, isn't it?' she said. 'Is that why you're refusing to look at me?'

Charlene swung round, and Laura saw that it was embarrassment, not fever, that was making her friend stumble over her words. 'Laura, I — you're not — I mean, do you mind . . . ? Oh, dear.' She gulped and came to a stop.

'No,' said Laura quietly. 'I don't mind at all. You've been seeing Rodney, haven't you?'

'Not in the way you mean. But he has come to my house a few times — to teach me accounting. He's been very kind. I didn't tell you because I thought you mightn't like it . . . '

'You could have told me. I wouldn't have minded a bit,' Laura assured her, feeling a little guilty because she knew she ought to have minded. 'Are you going to go out with Rodney then, now that our engagement is off?'

Charlene nodded. 'Yes. He asked me last night. Oh, Laura, I'm so glad you're not mad at me . . . ' She paused and put a hand up to her mouth. 'You're not, are you?'

Laura shook her head. Rodney was a faster worker than she'd thought. But she wasn't mad. 'No,' she said. 'I'm glad. You'll suit him much better than I did. You have the kind of figure he admires. You like numbers and eating at home, and you don't want to go to college . . . ' She broke off because Charlene, lost in a dream world of Rodney, wasn't even pretending to listen.

That evening Laura told Lancelot that her engagement was over.

'Good,' said her father. 'Never did like that fellow. Much better off with young Adam.'

He broke into a cheerful rendition of 'Praise the Lord, the King of Heaven', and Laura said hastily, 'Dad, I don't like Adam, and he's certainly not interested in me.'

'Wouldn't be so sure of that.' Lancelot cleared his throat. 'Good man, Adam. Got guts.'

Now what was her father talking about? Did he really have some cockeyed dream that Adam was going to marry her and settle down? An enterprise for which he would need guts? She shook her head, not wanting to upset him, but seeing no sense in bolstering the illusion. 'I really don't like Adam, Dad,' she repeated.

They were standing beside the kitchen table, and when a voice from the doorway murmured, 'You're a fraud, Laura Allan,' she jumped and hit her hand on a chair.

'I am not,' she said indignantly. 'And you're a conceited oaf.'

'Now, now,' muttered Lancelot. 'Won't do, you know. Humph. Must be going. Promised to meet Primrose, you see.'

Before Laura could stop him, her father had sidled briskly out the door.

'He's leaving us to kiss and make up,' said Adam. 'Shall I oblige?'

'Yes,' snapped Laura. 'You can oblige by moving yourself and your rattletrap car out of my house.'

'My car is neither in the house nor is it a rattletrap. And I have no intention of moving. I will, however, kiss you if you like. You look remarkably attractive when you're dying to throw a tantrum and stamp your feet.'

And he looked remarkably attractive draped against the counter in a thin gray T-shirt, with his legs apart and his hands shoved into the pockets of his jeans.

Laura didn't want to throw a tantrum, she wanted to throw herself at him and press her eager body against his length.

But she wasn't going to do it.

'I never throw tantrums,' she said coldly. 'But I wouldn't mind slapping your face.'

'Try it.' Suddenly he seemed several inches taller, and twice as menacing, and Laura knew that if she took him at his word she would regret it.

'Another time,' she said, backing down hastily. 'But I'm afraid you really can't stay.'

'Why can't I?' He shifted his thighs along the counter.

'Because I don't want you to.'

'You mean because I kissed you and woke you up,' he said flatly.

'Of course not. I — '

'You're a lousy liar, Miss Allan. You're terrified I'll kiss you again, and that you'll find yourself in the position of having to admit you enjoy it. As you did last night.'

'I did not . . . ' She broke off when she saw him curl his lip in what might

166

have passed for a smile if she hadn't known better.

Adam *expected* her to deny it.

'Yes. I did enjoy it,' she agreed. 'But it was just a moment of madness at the end of a very fraught day. I certainly *wouldn't* enjoy it if it happened again.'

'Is that so?' Adam perched himself on a corner of the counter and spread his legs. 'Then we'll have to see that it doesn't happen, won't we?'

'It won't, because you won't be here,' said Laura. His posture was aggressively sexual, as she was sure he meant it to be, and already her knees were starting to feel limp.

'Oh, yes, I will. But apart from that I'm willing to fall in with your wishes. So from now on it's strictly hands-off. I'll keep my distance, and I won't make a single move that could conceivably lead to a kiss. Oh, and I certainly won't attempt to seduce you. Provided you don't attempt to seduce me. Will that do?'

No, it wouldn't do at all, Laura

realized. Her mouth had gone dry just looking at him. She wouldn't be able to bear living in the same house with Adam if he kept his hands off her. *Or* if he didn't. But seeing him every day, hearing him laugh, watching his beautiful body move across the room, and all the time knowing he wouldn't come near her, would be torture. Unendurable torture.

'No,' she said. 'You'll still have to go.'

He shook his head slowly, and a small, grim smile played at the edges of his mouth. 'You don't get it, do you?' he said. 'There's no question of my leaving. Your father has asked me to stay. My rent's paid till the end of July. After that I may reconsider.'

'But why?' Laura groaned. 'Why do you insist on staying where you're not wanted?'

'It's not a matter of whether I'm wanted, Laura. It's a matter of what I want.'

'Adam Veryan! You are the most impossibly arrogant man I've ever met — '

'I do my best,' he agreed laconically, and Laura knew he was trying to bait her into losing control. He seemed to enjoy making her squirm. Well, she wasn't going to. She would handle this situation with as much dignity as she could muster, and hope somehow to stay sane until the end of the month.

'Very well,' she said haughtily. 'I suppose I'll have to put up with you. But it won't be easy.'

'I don't mean it to be.' Adam stretched his arms lazily over his head, nodded to her, and sauntered out of the kitchen. Laura was left with a strong feeling that she'd lost not only the battle but the war.

For the next two weeks, Adam adhered rigidly to his promise.

During the day he was either out, or in the basement pounding away at his computer. He avoided breakfast until after Laura left for work, and on those occasions when he was asked to join the family for supper, he seemed abstracted. She had a feeling his abstraction was more than just a pose. Sometimes she caught him watching her with a strange, fierce look in his pirate's eyes. Other times he sat staring straight ahead, as if she didn't even exist. Was his writing forcing him to confront memories he would have preferred to leave buried?

Whatever the reason for it, Adam's lack of attention drove her crazy. But in spite of, or perhaps because of, his withdrawal, she was conscious all the time that he was *there*.

Occasionally, as she tried to study or cook meals, she wondered if he was emitting some kind of magnetic field. It was certainly true that however hard she tried, whenever he was in the room she couldn't keep her eyes off him. But then she had known it would be like this from the moment he had insisted on staying.

One night, as she lay sleepless on her bed, Laura heard Adam and Lancelot returning from the Cinnamon Arms. Lancelot was singing a song which, fortunately, it never occurred to him to sing around the house. Adam was accompanying him in a deep, haunting baritone which for some inexplicable reason brought tears to Laura's eyes.

It was on a cool and cloudy Saturday two days later that Laura, who was already restless and on edge, became aware of a rhythmic humming noise drifting up through the floor beneath her feet.

'That's all I need,' she muttered. 'Flying saucers doing repairs in my basement.' And then, because she had acquired a habit of blaming Adam for everything disruptive in her life, 'What in the world are you doing now, Adam Veryan?'

When nobody answered, she pursed her lips and marched down the stairs to put a stop to whatever was going on.

The noise was louder down here, a whining warning of trouble. Adam's door was ajar, so it didn't come from there after all. Laura pushed her way past a clutter of boxes, two chairs with no seats, a rusted metal trunk and a picture with its face to the wall. She turned the picture round, discovered it was Great-aunt Deborah looking disapproving, and turned it back. Then, behind a pile of magazines depicting well-endowed ladies in precarious states of undress — Ethan was growing up fast, she thought resignedly — she discovered the flying saucer's command post. It was an old radio whose alarm had been accidentally set. At least she had to assume it was an accident, because Ethan wouldn't have deliberately drawn attention to his cache.

'Or would he?' she muttered, as Howard, disturbed from his rest, began a squeaking follow-up to the radio's serenade.

'Stuff it, Howard,' murmured a sleepy voice from Adam's inner sanctum.

Howard obliged with a full-throated oratorio, and Laura murmured a word she rarely used and flung wide the half-open door.

The curtains were drawn back from the small window, and a pale gray light lit the practically furnished room. Howard, in a cage against the wall, continued his enthusiastic warbling, and in the dimness Laura could just make out Adam's shape on the bed. She flipped the light on, but he didn't stir.

'Are you all right?' she asked, with more irritation than concern. It wasn't like Adam to fall asleep during the day.

When he didn't answer, and she thought she heard the sound of gentle snoring, she moved cautiously across the carpet to stand beside him.

Not cautiously enough.

As she frowned worriedly down at the bed, Adam's arm snaked out and caught her around the hips. She struggled frantically to maintain her balance, raised her arms, and a second later found herself upside down across a warm and very muscular male body.

Howard's oratorio rose to high C, and ended in a deafening silence.

6

'Oh! Adam, what do you think you're . . . ?' Laura broke off. Whatever Adam thought he was doing, he was probably right. And it was up to her to stop him. 'Your hands are on me,' she snapped, stating the obvious, and wishing she didn't want those hands to stay exactly where they were.

'Mmm. So they are,' he agreed drowsily, tightening his hold.

'But you promised.'

'Hmm? What did I promise?' She felt his body shift lazily underneath her, and when she lifted her head to look down at him she saw that he was only half awake and enticingly naked from the waist up.

'That you would keep your hands *off* me,' she said sharply.

'Oh.' He sounded disappointed. 'I might have known it was only a dream.'

'What was a dream?' She realized she was still draped over him in a compromising if delicious position, and began to struggle to get up.

'That you were standing beside my bed, smiling an invitation — '

'I was standing beside your bed, but I wasn't smiling any invitation.' She stopped struggling then and paused to look at him more closely. There was something odd about his normally dark skin. In places it appeared almost green. And his eyes were only half open. 'Adam, have you been drinking?'

'Certainly not,' he replied, raising heavy lids with what appeared to be an effort. The look he gave her was lazily sardonic. 'I am merely sleeping off the effects of a restless night.'

'Oh. Why were you restless? Are you ill? You do look a bit green.'

'Do I? In that case I hope Martians are in this year. Are you attracted to Martians, Laura?'

'No,' replied Laura. She frowned. Although Adam was laughing at her as usual, there were deep shadows under his eyes. He looked bruised, exhausted with a weariness that ran deeper than mere lack of sleep.

'Is it the book?' she asked, struggling out of his grasp and sitting up. 'Does writing it reopen old wounds?'

'Why should it?' He turned his face to the wall.

'I don't know. I thought — '

'You thought war was glamorous and exciting. Which, from the comfortable perspective of Cinnamon Bay, no doubt it is.'

Oh. So it *was* the book. 'No,' she said. 'I've read your columns. There's nothing glamorous about getting shot at and watching people die.'

'What do you know about it?' He rolled over on his back and looked up at her with a lifetime of cynicism in his eyes. 'There are a lot of things besides bullets that make war hell.'

'I can't change the fact that I haven't lived in your shoes,' said Laura, controlling her resentment only because she understood that Adam was using her lack of experience as a way of fighting his own demons. 'But I'll listen if you like.'

Adam lifted a hand and twisted it in the loose fall of her hair. 'You'll listen, will you?' he mimicked. 'You want to hear about nights under the stars, the camaraderie of shared danger, the high when it's all over and you're still alive? Or do you want the reality, which is heat, dust and mosquitoes, the smell of death, freezing nights, and the terrible silence that can sometimes follow the sounds of pitched battle? Which do you want, Laura? The pretty fantasy or the unholy truth?'

He was pulling her hair, hurting her scalp, but she didn't think he was aware of what he was doing. 'Neither,' she said firmly. 'I want to know why you do what you do, why you're writing about it when reliving the memories is so painful.'

'Ah.' He dropped his hand and made a sound that might have been a laugh or a groan. 'Do you, now? All right, Miss

Ministering Angel, I started out doing it because the paper I worked for in those days sent me to cover a minor rebellion in South America. Being green and inexperienced, I managed to get myself taken hostage. When I escaped, I wrote about it. The articles were a success. In the end, the only assignments I got seemed to involve fun stuff with gunfire and bombs.' His mouth angled down in a sneer. 'Besides, someone has to do it. The world needs to know that men can be blind, stupid idiots. As well as heroes. That's why I mean to finish this damn book.'

Laura nodded, understanding fully for the first time that there was more to this arrogant, sometimes merciless man than she had thought. More, perhaps, than he wanted her to see.

'Yes, I see,' she said. And then, sensing that Adam needed to be jolted out of the grim, forbidding humour that was keeping him awake at nights, she bent down and dropped a quick kiss on his lips.

Something sharp and very physical flared in his eyes, and just before he shot out an arm to clamp it around her waist and pull her over him she saw his chest muscles contract.

'What are you doing?' she gasped, as he moved his hips very explicitly. She felt as if an ember that had been glowing inside her ever since she had come into Adam's room had flared up and burst into flame.

'Teaching you the consequences of kissing me,' he replied, running a hand slowly down her back and over her bottom. 'Mmm. Very nice,' he added, giving it an approving pat.

Laura realized that her efforts to channel his thoughts away from the pain of the past had succeeded altogether too well.

'Don't,' she groaned, as the heat became almost unbearable. 'Don't, Adam. You promised.'

'So I did,' he agreed, lifting his hips again. 'All right, blue-eyes, never say I'm not a man of my word.'

She was still lying across him, limp now and incapable of resistance, when he put both hands on her waist, and with a swift motion lifted her off the bed and on to her feet. Then he rose too, and began to fasten the belt on black jeans which accentuated the taut outline of his thighs.

Laura murmured a quick prayer under her breath and moved away from him.

'Did you say what I think you said?' he asked, snapping the belt into place. 'It sounded encouraging.'

She stared at his broad, naked chest then raised her eyes to his face. Dear lord, he was gorgeous. And Martians might not be in this year, but surely this devastating pirate was? She took a half-step forward, then remembered that this was the careless heartbreaker who had arrogantly meddled in her life. In doing so he had chalked up another casual conquest for himself before moving on to greener pastures and more worldly, sophisticated women.

Adam had made it more than clear that although he found her mildly amusing, and not unattractive, she was not his kind of woman. Nor, she suspected, would any woman hold his interest for long. He didn't stay in one place long enough to form attachments.

'It wasn't meant to be encouraging,' she said. 'I'm sorry I disturbed you.'

'Yes,' he said softly. 'You do disturb me. Considerably more than I expected. And very bad for my beauty sleep it's proving. But don't worry. I plan to get my own back.'

You already have, thought Laura despairingly. She gave him a black look, and when he laughed and started to move towards her she turned to run up the stairs. She couldn't bear to be in the room with him any longer.

Behind her, she heard Adam's smoky laughter, and Howard humming ominously in his cage.

I'll never be able to stand it, she thought, collapsing at the kitchen table and burying her head in her hands. I hate Adam Veryan, he's an overbearing, self-satisfied chauvinist with itchy feet. Even if he does write wonderful columns, even though he *cares* about what he writes, he's the last man on earth I'd want to get involved with. She gave a low groan. And all he has to do is look at me with those horrible bedroom eyes of his and I turn into a mindless lump of putty. How am I ever going to survive until he leaves?

She reached for a mug of coffee that wasn't there.

That night Adam appeared uninvited at the dinner table. When his gaze swept appraisingly over her figure in a neat summer dress, as it had done that first day in the kitchen, she knew at once that everything had changed — that the peaceful days when he had behaved as if she were near invisible were at an end.

They were. From that day on, Adam no longer left her to eat breakfast in peace and private, but sat across the table from her looking casually virile and immovable. She knew he was aware that his presence unnerved her, and in the evenings, when she left her studies to cook a meal, he would often turn up to lounge in the kitchen doorway. As she bustled about chopping and stirring, he would watch her every move with hooded, darkly disturbing eyes. He reminded her of a vampire trying to decide whether or not he fancied her for lunch. Sometimes Laura wondered if he guessed how close he came to ending up as the base for one of her stews.

It seemed as though the end of the month would never come.

It did of course, but not, as she had hoped, to the accompaniment of Adam's departure. Instead she came home from work on the last day of July to find Lancelot standing in the middle of the living-room happily pocketing a cheque.

'What's that for?' she asked suspiciously.

'Adam's August rent,' replied her father.

'But you can't — he can't — I mean, Adam's not staying,' she stuttered.

'Course he is. Need someone to keep an eye on you and Ethan while I'm away. Don't I, Adam?' He turned to the cause of the dispute, who was settled comfortably in an armchair with the paper.

'Of course,' agreed Adam, stretching his long legs and looking up from an article on Cinnamon Bay's new drainage system. 'Laura needs a bit of supervision.' His eyes supervised her very specifically over the top of the paper, and she tried to decide whether to kick him hard and immediately, or wait for revenge until she had a chance to put hot mustard in his soup.

Then both options faded from her mind, as the import of her father's words sank in.

'Dad — what did you mean about needing someone here 'when you're away'? You never go away.' When he didn't answer at once, but stared at the empty brick fireplace and began to shuffle his feet, she lifted a hand to her mouth. 'You're not going into hospital, are you?'

'Certainly not.' Lancelot emphatically shook his head. 'Healthy as a horse. Going to Vancouver to meet a couple of old friends from the regiment. And their wives.' His gaze slid away from her and he added gruffly, 'Primrose has agreed to come with me.'

Laura's eyes widened. So her father and Primrose de Vere were going on holiday together. She smiled, for a moment forgetting what this conversation was all about. It would be good for her father to have someone of his own when she left for college . . .

When she . . . No. College wasn't the issue right now. Nor was Primrose. Laura swallowed, groped for the back of a wicker chair and sank into it. The issue was the velvet-eyed devil her father was calmly proposing to leave her with while he trundled off to Vancouver.

'When did all this come up, Dad?'

she asked, in a voice that those who knew her well would have recognized as not nearly as composed as it sounded.

'Couple of weeks ago. Forgot to tell you.'

Sure you did, thought Laura. Because if you *had* told me, I'd have insisted that Adam was out of the house before you could pocket his rent.

She curled her fingers round the arms of the chair and breathed in. Hard. How *could* her father, who loved her dearly, have been so gullible as to imagine that Adam's intentions, if he had any, were anything but dishonorable? He seemed to have some crazy idea that the man might actually be willing to marry her.

'I'm glad you're going to have a holiday, Dad,' she said to Lancelot. 'But obviously Adam can't stay here while you're gone.' She spoke slowly, in a calm, matter-of-fact tone that she hoped might penetrate her father's single-minded refusal to see what he didn't want to see. He had always been like that, she reflected. He'd lost his wife because he wouldn't admit he could see the obvious. And, even as she spoke, Laura knew her attempt to change his habit of a lifetime was doomed to fail.

'Course he can,' Lancelot responded offhandedly. 'Ethan will be here. Besides . . . ' His blue eyes twinkled with triumph. 'You haven't spoken a civil word to Adam in weeks. No danger of your getting up to mischief.'

Oh, thought Laura. The plot thickens. Dad imagines that if I'm left on my own with Adam, sooner or later hormones will get the better of me and I'll tumble happily into his arms. My poor, deluded father. He actually believes that if I did tumble, Adam would go no further than a kiss. Not that the arm-tumbling part was entirely beyond the realms of possibility, she acknowledged with an inward sigh. Look what had happened at the Sanctuary.

She glanced at Adam, still calmly

reading the paper. Perhaps, after all, she was wrong. Adam had shown no real interest in her, beyond the casual sport of driving her crazy. And yet there had been times when she could have sworn he wasn't as detached as he made out. There *was* a kind of chemistry between them, even though it mostly manifested itself in Adam's provocation, and her determination to provoke him back.

Her resolve stiffened. 'Ethan won't be the least bit of good as a chaperone,' she told her father flatly. 'He'll be off pursuing frogs and things all the time.'

'Don't need a chaperon.' Lancelot refused to budge from his position. 'Adam's a gentleman. Aren't you, Adam?'

Adam lowered the article on drains and shook his head. 'No,' he admitted, with his crooked, heart-stopping smile. 'I'm afraid I'm not. But I promise you I won't seduce your daughter.'

'Hah.' Lancelot gave a short bark of laughter. 'Good enough for me.'

'Well, it isn't good enough for me,' said Laura, making a superhuman effort not to shout.

'Come, come. You're a modern young woman, my dear. Wouldn't like to think of you on your own, though. Prowlers and all that . . . '

'Dad,' said Laura, exasperated, 'the only prowler who's ever shown up around here is Larry Lovejoy — and Pal barked so hard he ran away.' She turned to the tan and white dog who had just bustled into the room. 'Didn't you, Pal?'

Pal trotted over to Adam and offered a paw.

'Traitor,' muttered Laura.

Adam put down his paper, accepted the paw, and raised an eyebrow at Laura. 'You're outnumbered,' he told her. 'I have your brother's vote as well.'

'I wouldn't doubt it,' she muttered, thinking that no man had a right to such sexy eyebrows.

Adam shook his head at her and asked softly, almost as if he'd read her thoughts, 'Do I make you nervous, blue-eyes?'

'Of course not.' Laura tossed her head and a curtain of red hair tumbled in front of her face. When she brushed it back, she saw that Adam was once more absorbed in the details of the town's drainage system.

Lancelot's gaze shifted from the top of Adam's head to his daughter's fingers strumming indignantly on her knee. 'Have to pack,' he said abruptly, and hurried out of the room.

Laura watched his strategically departing back with resignation. How different her father had been these past few weeks. More cheerful and less inclined to grumble. She had put the change down to Adam's dubious influence, but it was beginning to look as though it had more to do with Primrose de Vere.

She turned back to Adam, who was absently fondling Pal's ear as he continued his perusal of the paper. 'You don't make me in the least nervous,' she repeated, with a lofty absence of truth.

'Prove it.' He went on reading.

'What? What do you mean?'

He didn't even trouble to raise his head. 'Stop searching for excuses to make me leave.'

'Excuses? I don't need excuses.' She glared at him and got no response. 'All right, if *you* won't go, *I'll* leave. You can stay here and look after Ethan.'

'And where do you plan to go?' asked Adam, but not as if he particularly cared.

'To Charlene's.' Laura gave the first answer she could think of.

'Mmm. Interesting.'

'And what's *that* supposed to mean?' She didn't trust that quiver in his voice.

'The noble Rodney, of course.' He turned a page. 'I hear Charlene has collected your leftovers.'

Laura bit her lip. It was true that Charlene and Rodney had become an item. And she was glad for them. 'Rodney was never my leftover,' she said sharply. 'And don't worry, I'll find somewhere to go.'

Abruptly Adam dropped his paper to the floor, startling the drowsy dog at his feet. 'Come here,' he said.

When Laura didn't move, he leaned forward, caught her wrists and pulled her in between his knees. 'Now,' he ordered, 'tell me I don't make you nervous.'

Laura looked him straight in the eye. 'You don't make me nervous,' she said. And it was true. At this moment she was only afraid of herself, of the treacherous desires of a body that was straining to fall into his arms, to feel his lean length against her softness.

'Fine,' said Adam, interrupting this disturbing train of thought. 'Then since the proprieties will be observed by Ethan's presence, there isn't a reason in the world why I shouldn't stay. Is there?'

'But I don't want you to,' groaned Laura, horribly conscious of her bare legs pressing against the tight denim stretched across his thighs.

'I know, and that's just too bad, blue-eyes.' He slid his hands up to her elbows. 'Because you and I, my fiery little iceberg, are about to start playing house.'

Laura closed her eyes. 'Why, Adam?' she demanded. 'Why do you insist — ?'

He shrugged. 'Why not? It suits me to stay here.'

Staring at the rock hard line of his jaw, Laura knew she had lost. 'Maybe it does. But that promise you made to my father . . . '

Adam smiled, although his eyes didn't. 'Don't get your hopes up. It's a promise I don't plan to break.'

'I think,' said Laura slowly, through her teeth, 'that one of us must be going mad.'

'Very likely.' With no warning at all Adam pulled her on to his knee and wrapped a firm arm around her waist. 'The question is, *which* one of us? Now let's see. If I were to touch you just here . . . ' He laid his palm over her left thigh. 'And then here . . . ' He shifted it up her leg, and a terrifying warmth swept up from her toes to the very tops of her ears. 'And then here — '

'Adam,' cried Laura. 'Adam, please . . .'

He stopped at once, and an odd look came into his eyes. As if a light-hearted game had suddenly acquired darker, more dangerous undertones.

'I'm sorry,' he said curtly. 'That was uncalled for.'

'Yes, but — Adam, what *do* you want from me?'

What she wanted from him was that he continue his erotic explorations. She knew she ought to escape at once from the mind- and body-drugging clutches of this man, but she was unable to summon the will to do it.

'Nothing,' he said, abruptly tipping her off his knee. 'I want absolutely nothing from you, Laura.'

Laura straightened her skirt. 'In that case,' she said quietly, 'why do you insist on trying to drive me crazy?'

'Damned if I know. Because you make it so easy, I suppose.' Adam's clipped tone didn't match the flippant response, and his oblique smile was quite unlike his usual slash of a grin. To Laura, he seemed like a man who had encountered an unexpected and unwelcome obstacle which he resented but intended to overcome. Briefly, she wondered if *she* could be the obstacle, then dismissed the notion. She had shown him in a hundred different ways that, if he put his mind to seduction, her resistance would be pathetically ineffective.

Which was why she couldn't stay in this house with only Ethan and a dog between her and total insanity. Left to herself, she was more likely to attempt to seduce Adam than the other way around. She couldn't face that. The humiliation if — *when* he rejected her would be too great.

'If you insist on staying, I *am* leaving,' she told him, standing very tall and holding her palms flat against her thighs.

'Ah. So you *are* frightened of me.' He smiled again in that way she didn't like.

'No,' she insisted. 'I'm not. I just don't want you to stay.' She wasn't about to tell him that the only person she was afraid of was herself.

'Coward.' His voice was silky, cutting, and Laura felt a painful stab of anger. She wasn't a coward. She was confused, resentful and unhappy, but not in the least frightened of Adam Veryan. And if the only way she could prove it . . .

'All right,' she heard herself saying. 'You can stay if you must. Just make sure you stay out of my way.'

'And if I don't?' Adam tilted his head lazily against the back of the chair.

'I'll — I'll — '

'Devise seven ways to make my life hell?' he suggested, correctly divining the direction of her thoughts. 'Don't waste your time. I've had a lot more experience with hell than you have. And don't stamp your feet,' he added, as she turned her back and made for the door.

Laura clenched her teeth. She had never stamped her feet in her life, and she didn't appreciate being spoken to as if she were about to enter her second childhood. But she knew she would certainly act like a child if she attempted to respond to him now, because her fingers were just itching to scratch his face.

Lips pressed together, she marched out of the room and up the stairs.

The following evening, when she came home from work, she was in time to see Lancelot departing in a flurry of suitcases, golf clubs and last-minute forays into the house to collect forgotten photographs and 'that book I borrowed from Old Leversage ten years ago'. Finally, with a plump and smiling Primrose in tow, he climbed into the family's ancient Ford and bumped off down the road singing a rousing chorus of 'Onward Christian Soldiers'. As Laura waved him off, she thought wryly that if Primrose de Vere survived this week-long test of her stamina, she was almost certain to become the second Mrs Allan.

Adam, who had been standing in the doorway, came up behind Laura and looped a casual arm around her waist. 'Just the two of us now,' he murmured, giving her thigh an incendiary little pat.

'Except for Ethan, Pal, two cats, a guinea pig and assorted rodents,' said Laura dampingly. But she didn't push away his arm, because she liked the feel of it there.

Adam shook his head. 'The fur brigade maybe, but not Ethan. Didn't your father tell you?'

'Tell me what?' asked Laura, trying to sound unconcerned, but suspecting she only sounded anxious.

'That Ethan has left to stay with his friend in Victoria.'

'He can't have. Howard and the gang are still here.' Laura clutched at this fact as if it were her only hope of salvation from a headlong descent into . . . No, not hell. More likely Adam's bed. Which, judging from his reputation, would probably be anything but hell. All the same, she wasn't about to find out.

'*I'm* looking after the menagerie while your brother's gone,' explained Adam, effectively dashing her hopes. She didn't miss the undercurrent of amusement, and had to conquer an uncharacteristic urge to scream.

A warm breeze blew up off the sea, lifting her hair and, strangely, making her shiver. She became aware of Adam's fingers tapping out a rhythm on her thigh, and immediately tried to push him away. 'Dad wouldn't forget . . . ' she began. Then stopped. Because of course Dad would.

Lancelot, in his way, was a lot like Adam. If he wanted something, he had no qualms or conscience about how he went about getting it. In this case he wanted Adam for his daughter, and had it obstinately fixed in his head that all he had to do to achieve this goal was leave them alone together for a week. She supposed that if she were Ethan's Aphrodite, and Adam were

Demetrius, it might work.

But she wasn't Aphrodite. And her unprincipled but loving father had, with the best of intentions, left her alone in the house with a man whose very presence was an addiction.

It was too much. She had to get away.

Abruptly, and without so much as a backward glance at Adam, Laura twisted away from him and turned to go into the house. When she heard his footsteps behind her, she slammed the door on him and ran as fast as she could out back. From there she hurried into the enclosing safety of the woods.

At once her mood changed, as tension and resentment dropped away. These woods had been her refuge since childhood. It was here she had come to mourn the death of her mother, and in an age when children were often told not to walk alone in dark places, she had never for a moment felt in danger. Here there was only tranquility and healing, and the occasional raccoon or nervous deer.

Automatically Laura's feet led her along a carpet of pine needles to her secret place deep among the trees where, in a small, moss-covered clearing, a narrow stream glimmered over gray and white pebbles before whispering its way down to the sea. With a thankful sigh, she sank on to the ground and watched the water shimmering over the stones.

Peace at last. Even if it was only a temporary peace. She stared into the stream and allowed her mind to go blank.

It seemed only a few seconds later that she sensed another presence in the glade, and realized she was no longer alone. She turned, expecting to encounter the bespectacled eyes of a raccoon, or perhaps a rabbit. Instead she found herself gazing at a man's bare leg. A very familiar leg with a small scar just above the ankle. A leg that belonged to the one person she most particularly wanted to avoid.

'I came here to get away from you,' she said. 'To be by myself so I could think.'

'About me?' he asked, his voice grating on the words.

Why deny it? 'Yes. About you,' she agreed.

'A waste of your time again, blue-eyes.' He flung himself down on the moss. 'I'm not your ticket to escape from the monotony of life in Cinnamon Bay.'

Laura ran her eyes quickly over the firm body sprawled so unselfcon-sciously beside her, and found herself longing to reach out to unbutton his shirt, to run her hands across his chest and down the flat expanse of his abdomen. Then the unfairness of his words sank in, and she discovered that the magic of the woods didn't work when Adam was around. She no longer felt tranquil and benign.

'I don't find Cinnamon Bay monoto-nous,' she snapped. 'And even if I were looking for a ticket out, surely you don't think I'd accept it in the form of the most impossibly self-satisfied, interfering, overbearing toad I've ever met. I expect to do much better than that.'

Not a muscle on Adam's face moved. 'Thank you.' He nodded gravely. 'What else am I?'

'Isn't that enough?' asked Laura, most of the steam knocked out of her by the bleakness in his eye.

'No. And you, Laura Allan, are a fraud, as I've mentioned before.' He picked up a lock of her long hair and twisted it around his fist. Then with a little tug he pulled her face down until it was hovering just above his, and said softly, 'You also want very much for me to take you to bed. Which must make you one of those women who favour self-satisfied, interfering, overbearing men. Too bad for you.'

'I don't — I'm not . . . ' began Laura. But it was too late, because his fingers were at her waist, sliding under the waistband of her skirt, and when she made a soft sound in her throat he put his free hand on her neck and dragged her down beside him on the moss. A second later his lips had closed conclusively over hers.

At once she was overwhelmed by the helpless, drowning sensation she always experienced in Adam's arms. But this time some speck of sanity remained, and she remembered how their love-making had ended in the past — with Adam pulling away and leaving her with a figurative pat on the head. As if she were some virginal ingénue who wasn't old enough to be treated as a woman. But as his kiss deepened, and she felt the pressure of his hand down her thigh and his bare legs tangling erotically with hers, she vowed that this time *she* would be the one to end it.

When he moved to pull her on top of him, she squirmed away and sprang to her feet. It took her a few moments to catch her breath.

Adam stared up at her with an enigmatic glitter in his eyes, but he made no attempt to drag her back. Nor did he trouble to get up.

'What's the matter, Laura?' he taunted, folding his hands behind his head. 'Afraid we won't make it to the bed?'

'Oh,' she gasped. 'Of all the — no, Adam, hard as it may be for you to accept, I'm not interested in making it to your bed. You may remember I plan to save that for the man I marry. *If* I marry.'

'Then that lucky fellow will have his hands full.' Adam was caustic. 'And don't worry, I'll be keeping my promise to your father. I've never taken an unwilling woman in my life, and I sure as hell don't aim to start with you.'

Laura clenched her fists. Once again Adam had managed to make her feel as if she were too young to be initiated into the mysteries of adult lovemaking. And yet he had called her a woman — kissed her as a woman . . . So why did he persist in tormenting her? Did it amuse him to prove again and again that she hadn't the power to resist him? Was that what this was all about? Power? Or did he have some other end in mind?

She gazed down at him as he sat up unhurriedly and propped his back against a tree-trunk. Lord, he was attractive, she thought despairingly. And if he did have something in mind besides an unkind amusement, she might as well find out what it was.

'Or I with you,' she assured him, tossing her head. When he only continued to gaze at her with that maddening glitter, she scuffed the moss with her toe and snapped, 'What *is* it you want from me, Adam?'

'Bed. And breakfast, my sweet.'

'But you promised my father you wouldn't — wouldn't — '

'Seduce you?' His laugh was harsh. 'That's right, I won't. Although I'm beginning to think a thorough seduction may be exactly what you want.'

Laura planted her hands on her hips.

'I see,' she said, in a voice that dripped acid. 'So you're one of those ridiculous men who thinks all any woman needs to make her happy is a good stud. Are you a good stud, Adam?'

For a moment she wasn't sure if he wanted to laugh or shake her, but she had the satisfaction of knowing she had taken him by surprise. Then, before she could move, he was on his feet, and his big hands were gripping her shoulders.

'Do you want to find out?' he asked her. His voice was deceptively casual.

She swallowed. 'Find out what?'

'How good a stud I am, of course.'

The heat triggered by his words and by his touch rose up to suffuse her face with fire. 'No,' she said desperately. 'No, Adam, I don't. I just want to know why you're doing this. Why you've been going out of your way to torment me. You say you don't want me — '

'Oh, I want you,' he corrected her. 'What I said was that I didn't plan to have you. I still don't. You're too young and too bedazzled by dangerous illusions about my lifestyle. And I do have the remnants of a conscience.'

Laura gazed up into the darkness of his eyes. They were the sort of eyes a woman could easily drown in if she weren't careful. And he had said he wanted her. But as she saw the muscles tighten around his mouth she remembered that he had also said she was too young and too bedazzled. Not his sort of woman. Just someone to tease and provoke because she always rose so nicely to the bait.

'So you don't want anything from me,' she said slowly. 'Literally nothing beyond a place to sleep and breakfast.' When she felt his fingers bite into her shoulders, she added almost to herself, 'Will you ever want more from anyone, I wonder?'

Adam narrowed his eyes. 'Love, for instance?' He gave a scornful laugh. 'What a romantic little innocent you are. Oh, I believe in it, mind you. I've seen incredible sacrifices made in the name of love. But it's not for me, pretty blue-eyes. Not now, and maybe not ever. I haven't either the time or the inclination.'

7

A twig snapped under an animal's soft tread somewhere in the woods behind them. Laura felt as if her neck were frozen at its current angle, her eyes locked forever with Adam's.

Love? Why was Adam talking about love? She hadn't meant — or had she?

Oh, God. She closed her eyes so she couldn't see the blank disillusionment in his.

Confusion. Bewilderment. Disbelief. Desire too, as well as the beginnings of anger. Surely to heaven she wasn't in love with Adam? Why, only a few weeks ago she had been engaged to dependable, conservative Rodney. She *couldn't* love Adam, the risk-taker, who had a reputation for changing women as often as his clothes. This wasn't a man who would ever settle down to domesticity, and any woman foolish enough to love him would regret it.

So why was she even thinking about love?

'Adam,' said Laura, opening her eyes. 'It doesn't matter to me whether you're capable of love or not. Obviously a man as footloose as you are can't afford to be tied down to one woman. Is that why you lost your Christine? Because you couldn't, or wouldn't, take her with you?'

'Couldn't *and* wouldn't,' Adam said harshly. 'Laura, can't you get it into your head that my work is no package holiday?'

Laura had to bite back the anger that had been so close to the surface ever since he had interrupted her quiet reverie in the glade. Anger and something else, she thought grimly, as he slid a hand under her hair and his touch sent its inevitable shivers down her spine. But there was no point in shouting at him, and it wasn't her way to lose control.

'And can't you get it into *your* head,'

she replied, 'that I've never regarded danger as the ultimate high? Yes, there have been times when I've dreamed of adventure, but I see no adventure in sharing my bed with a man who will love me and leave me the moment he catches the faintest scent of a battle in some far-off corner of the globe. So it's just as well you weren't planning to have me, isn't it? Because I certainly wasn't planning to have you. Why would I? I don't even like you very much.' She wriggled her shoulders, and Adam let her go just as a sunbeam broke through the dark green foliage overhead to lighten his face with its gold.

A muscle pinched the corner of his mouth, and suddenly he looked older, harder, as if she had hit some nerve he didn't want exposed. 'Yes, you've made that unflatteringly clear from the beginning,' he answered. 'On the other hand, I've noticed that in some respects you're not entirely bored with my — '

'Charms again?' queried Laura sweetly.

'What charms, Adam?'

He shrugged, and rested his shoulders against the rough bark of a fir tree. 'You really are anxious to find out, aren't you?' he said conversationally. 'In fact you almost tempt me to show you. But as you've assured me you're saving your particlar charms for the man you marry — that would put me in a difficult situation. Wouldn't it?'

'No,' said Laura. 'It would put *me* in a difficult situation.'

Adam smiled ambiguously and stuck his thumbs into his belt. 'I suppose it would,' he agreed. 'Unless I married you.'

Laura gulped, and caught her lip in her teeth to stop herself from gaping. 'Married?' she repeated. 'But you wouldn't — you don't — I mean you said you hadn't the time or inclination.'

'For love? True, but we were talking about marriage, my sweet, not love.'

Laura stared at him. His face was closed, like a book that had yet to be opened. 'You don't want marriage,' she said finally.

'How do you know? I'm thirty-five years old, Laura. Have you ever wondered what happens to used war correspondents when their bodies start to slow down?'

'No,' said Laura, who couldn't imagine that particular body ever slowing down. It was far too fit, and ready to pounce on susceptible females. And the wound in his leg had almost healed.

Adam laughed, a low, joyless laugh that made her flinch. 'To the point, as usual. But the fact remains that one day I'll have to give it up. And maybe when that day comes I'll decide I want a wife — along with a mother for my children.'

He didn't mean it. She could tell from the slant of his mouth and cynical droop of his eyelids.

Laura took up the challenge.

'I see,' she said, clasping her hands demurely at her waist. 'You mean that

Adam Veryan, free spirit and adventurer, may finally succumb to the primitive urge to perpetuate his genes. Now tell me — if that unlikely day ever comes, why should I be the lucky lady you decide to honour as the bearer of your posterity? Do I look like some sort of heifer?'

Adam put his head on one side and looked her up and down exactly as if he were contemplating the purchase of a cow. 'No. You look like an obstinate, elusive young woman with dazzling red hair who . . . ' He broke off as Laura turned her back and bent down to fasten her shoe. 'Who is presenting me with a very tempting proposition,' he finished.

'It doesn't tempt me at all,' said Laura, straightening at once and spinning round. 'When I marry, which won't be for a very long time, I'll want a husband I can love and depend on. A husband who will be there when I need him. Who will want more from me than children and . . . ' She hesitated.

'Sex?' Adam finished for her, his face expressing only polite interest.

'Yes.' She nodded, firmly suppressing a blush.

'How fortunate I didn't make you an offer, then.' Adam didn't look in the least discomposed. 'And I wasn't talking about that sort of temptation.' His gaze flicked suggestively over her figure, and once again Laura was forced to dig her nails into her palms.

'You don't really care about anything or anyone but your job, do you?' she accused him. 'What are you going to do when it's over? Shoot yourself?'

'Nope. I've seen enough of shooting.' He closed his eyes briefly. 'As for what I'll do — I don't know yet. I haven't given it much thought.'

'Haven't you?' Laura didn't believe him.

'Not seriously.' His voice was so repressive that Laura guessed he had given the matter a great deal of thought, and didn't relish the idea of a career change.

'Christine,' she said, and it wasn't a question. Somehow she knew the mysterious Christine was connected with Adam's current train of thought. 'Did you love her, then?'

'Love her?' He gave a bark of laughter and lifted his eyes to the whispering greenery overhead. 'Yes, I suppose I did. I was very young.'

And, by implication, too old for such juvenile passions now. 'But she didn't love you?'

'Oh, Christine loved me. She wanted to marry me.' He waved a hand in the direction of the ocean. 'She proposed to me down there on the beach one memorable fall afternoon.'

Laura blinked. Adam wasn't clamming up as he usually did when the subject of Christine came up, but he sounded unnaturally cold. As if he needed to keep the memories frozen. To dull his pain? she wondered, feeling an unaccustomed stab of sympathy for this hard-bitten man, who so seldom allowed his true feelings to surface.

'What happened?' she asked. Somehow it was important that he tell her.

Adam lowered his head to pin her with a bleak, almost disbelieving gaze. 'Does it matter?'

'No, but — '

'But you want to know. Sorry to disappoint you, but there's no great mystery. Just the usual hurt feelings and grief.'

Laura sat down on the moss, hoping he would go on. After a moment, he did.

'We grew up together, Christine and I. Our parents were friends, and any summer they weren't off gallivanting in search of adventure we all came here for our holidays. Those were the good times.' He moved his shoulders as if to relieve the tension in his muscles. 'At least, they were for us kids. We were more used to being shipped off to summer camp. Then, when Christine was nineteen and I was twenty-one, we came alone for a weekend. Just the two of us.' His mouth turned down. 'I'd never made love to her before but, with the arrogance of youth, I had always assumed Christine was mine and nobody else's.'

The arrogance of *youth*, thought Laura. Things haven't changed much then, have they? But she didn't say it.

'On the first day,' Adam continued, 'we went for a walk on the beach. And Christine asked me when we were going to get married. I was horrified. I'd just got my first job with the paper, and I knew I'd soon be posted overseas. I wasn't interested in marriage, but I was certain Christine would be there for me whenever I happened to come home.' He paused to break a twig off the tree. 'So I told her marriage was out of the question. She said it *was* the question, and that she couldn't wait around for years, never knowing when, or if, I'd come back to her. But if we were married, she said, of course it would make all the difference. I didn't believe she meant it, didn't believe she'd ever leave me, and I wasn't about to tie myself down.' He snapped the twig in half and tossed it on to the ground. 'Even when she refused to make love with me, I never doubted for a moment that once she got over her fit of pique she would be there, mine for the taking.'

'But she wasn't.' Laura ran her palm over the soft cushion of the moss and didn't look at him.

'No.' Adam's voice was grimly self-mocking. 'She had more sense. When I came back from that first assignment a year later, she had already married my sister's ex. She told me she'd done it so she wouldn't be tempted to wait for me — which did something for my ego but not a lot for my heart.'

'Was it broken?' asked Laura softly, wishing she could smooth the twisted outline of his mouth.

'Broken?' His laugh was a crack of contempt. 'I thought it was at the time. I couldn't believe Christine hadn't waited.' He shrugged. 'In the end, of course, I had no choice but to accept that I'd lost her. Much later I understood that she'd been right. I wouldn't have made her happy, I was far too wrapped up in myself and my career. And when I finally realized that, I made a decision.'

'Yes?' Laura looked up, hearing a new note in his voice, and to her confusion, although his eyes seemed far away, there was a small, oblique smile on his lips.

'Yes,' he said. 'I decided love and marriage were not for me.'

Laura tugged abstractedly at a tuft of bright green moss. 'And you still feel that way, of course,' she said flatly.

The smile grew even more oblique. 'Is there any reason I shouldn't?'

'No. No, of course not.'

'Then, as you say, of course I do.'

Laura frowned. There was that jeering note in his voice again and, as usual, he seemed bent on provoking her. She sensed that he was angry for some reason. It was almost as if, in a way, he wanted her to tell him that there *was* a reason for him to change his mind.

But there wasn't, she thought bewilderedly. And if she told him there was, he would laugh at her. He had already said that love and marriage were not for him. And if, one day, he did change his mind, she, Laura Allan from Cinnamon Bay, would never be the right woman for him. She couldn't possibly marry a man who was even more interfering than Rodney, and who had a woman in most of the major cities of the world . . .

'I'm going back to the house,' she said abruptly.

Adam's eyes gleamed at her from under the thick devil's eyebrows, and his teeth were a flash of white in golden bronze. 'So you don't want to marry me, Laura Allan. How very deflating.' He straightened slowly and stretched his arms over his head.

'Stop it,' snapped Laura. 'You know you don't mean it. And why would I even dream of marrying a man who takes such pleasure in tormenting me?'

'Tormenting you?' He took a step toward her. 'How do I torment you, Laura?'

Laura groaned silently and shut her eyes. But when she felt his breath lifting her hair, and caught the warm scent of his body close to hers, she forced herself to open them again.

Adam had placed a hand on the bark of the tree above her head. 'You know,' he murmured pensively, 'a man could do a lot worse. You're attractive. You're a passably efficient housekeeper. You like children. You're bright and quick — too damn quick sometimes.' His lips curled up in a disturbingly sensuous smile. 'And I think I would enjoy introducing you to certain pleasures your misguided Rodney appears to have overlooked. I've been told I'm a good teacher.'

'Oh,' gasped Laura, glaring at him. 'Oh! You conceited, smug, supercilious, self-satisfied *coxcomb*. If you think . . . '

She paused because, unaccountably, Adam's odd smile had turned into a frankly startled grin. And when he threw back his head to let out a roar of laughter, she stopped trying to speak altogether and placed her hands on her hips.

'Coxcomb?' he repeated, running his knuckles over her chin. 'Did you call me a *coxcomb*, Laura Allan?'

'Yes,' said Laura, the beginnings of a reluctant smile tugging at the edges of her mouth. 'It's Old English and it means a conceited fool.'

'I know what it means,' he said drily. 'That's what I like about you, blue-eyes. You know how to put a man in his place.'

'Yes,' agreed Laura. 'What I don't know is how to get him *out* of my place.'

'You've got that right,' he agreed. His mouth was turned down, but she could still see the amusement in his eyes, and when he put an arm around her waist to walk her back to the house, she didn't try to push him away. Her body felt surprisingly safe and warm against his side.

At least it did until they reached the back door, and she happened to glance up at Adam's profile. He was frowning, his mouth was flat, and as soon as he saw her looking at him, he turned away.

Laura, her thoughts in turmoil, pulled away from him and went straight into the kitchen to start supper.

As she chopped vegetables with unnecessary vigour, and threw in every spice on the rack, she was forced to acknowledge that Adam's talk of marriage, however ludicrous, disturbed her at some level deeper than mere irritation. In fact she found herself fighting a ridiculous inclination to cry.

Ten minutes later, as she was putting her creative casserole in the oven, she was startled to hear a stream of doubtful language coming through the wall from the garage. She closed the oven door and straightened warily. Now what? Had Ethan's pets mistaken Adam for a snack? Or was he just in an unusually foul mood?

A moment later she had her answer.

'Laura,' shouted Adam, slamming into the kitchen like a March wind. 'How good are you at delivering baby rats?'

Laura bit her lip. Adam's face was a lowering thundercloud, but she had an idea he was really more worried than angry. For once, she thought, with an uncharitable gloat of satisfaction, Mr Know-it-All doesn't have all the answers.

'I'm no good at all,' she told him bluntly. 'But I expect Aphrodite is. If I were you, I'd leave her alone to get on with it. She will anyway.'

Adam frowned. 'They're your brother's pets. Aren't you in the least bit concerned?'

'No. And if you'd lived with Ethan for fifteen years, you wouldn't be either.' Laura opened the fridge and pulled out a large head of cauliflower.

'Maybe not. But *I'm* responsible for young Ethan's damned zoo.'

'So you are,' Laura agreed smugly. 'And I wonder whose fault that is.' She picked up a saucepan and began to fill it with water.

The next moment she felt two firm hands grip her elbows. Then she was being propelled across the floor as if she were dust in front of a hurricane, and hustled out to the garage.

It only had one small window, and at first Laura couldn't see much in the soft rays cast by the evening sun. But as her eyes became used to the dimness she took in several cages, and saw that on a table in the nearest corner, Aphrodite was indeed giving birth — with the busy efficiency of an old hand at the job, which, for all Laura knew, she was.

'You see,' she said, triumphantly to Adam. 'I told you Aphrodite didn't need your help.'

'Well I'm damned.' Adam wasn't looking at her. Instead he was gazing down at the busy black and white mother as she bustled about the cage arranging her progeny of pulsing pink piles. 'Eleven of them. Good old Demetrius.' He glanced at another cage where Demetrius's pink nose protruded through the wire.

'I'd say Aphrodite had most to do with it,' said Laura caustically. 'Or do you have some sort of fellow feeling for a fellow rat?'

'Right,' said Adam. 'That does it.'

Before Laura could ask what did what, he had whipped her around and was moving her briskly through the door.

'Hey,' she cried, finding her voice. 'Let me go. You promised — '

'I didn't promise to put up with being called a rat.' He marched her across the hallway and up the stairs.

Help, thought Laura. Now what? I'm alone in the house with a mad pirate and a dog who thinks he's a rug. 'Pal!' she called hopefully. 'Pal, where are you?'

An outdoor rug, she thought disgustedly, when there was no answering patter of feet.

'Pal won't save you,' said Adam grimly. 'He's on my side.'

'Where — what are you doing?' Laura gasped, as Adam kicked open her bedroom door.

'Making you pay,' came the ominous reply. And then she was flat on her back on the bed, and Adam was leaning over her with both fists pressed into the pillow beside her head.

'You can't — you wouldn't . . . ' Laura wasn't sure whether to be frightened or angry, but she knew that if Adam didn't move away from her at once the question would soon become academic. She could smell the subtle man's scent of his skin, see the movement of muscles at his throat and the dark hair tumbling across his forehead. Hair that she longed to tangle through her fingers as she dragged his mouth down over hers . . .

And then, as she gazed up at him, hypnotized, she saw that the retaliatory glitter in his eyes had been replaced first by a gleam of surprise, and then by something darker, more intense.

'You were supposed to look terrified, not eager,' he said, sitting down on the bed beside her and straightening her skirt with a brisk, irritable motion.

'Why should I be terrified of you?' Laura smiled stoically. He did frighten her sometimes, but she wasn't going to let him know it. 'And anyway why would you *want* to terrify me?'

'Because I don't like being called a rat?' he suggested.

'Then don't act like one.'

'You don't learn, do you, Miss Allan?' The glitter was back in his eyes and he pinned her shoulders to the bed.

'Learn what?' she scoffed. 'To bow down to your every lordly whim?'

'That will do nicely for a start.'

'And if I don't?' She was *almost* sure he was teasing her. Almost but not quite.

'It depends on my mood.' He stood up suddenly and strode across to the window.

Laura gazed at his shoulders, at his

shirt so very white against the sky. There was something over-controlled and rigid about the way he was standing, as if at any moment he was likely to turn into the primitive creature she had always sensed lurked beneath the civilized veneer. This was a man who was used to doing what he wanted and taking what he wanted, with careless vitality and very little thought for the consequences.

Except, for some reason, when it came to her. He said he wanted her, and yet, when he could have done so, he hadn't taken her.

Laura frowned at his back, annoyed with herself for feeling a momentary pang of regret. 'What sort of mood are you in now?' she asked, trying not to let her voice betray her doubts.

He swung round and pressed his palms behind him on the sill. 'Frustrated,' he growled. 'Better beware, Laura Allan.'

Was he serious? It was never easy to tell with Adam.

'Then will you please go and be frustrated somewhere else?' she said. 'This happens to be *my* bedroom, in case you haven't noticed.'

'Oh, I've noticed.' He gave an exaggerated shudder, and when he lifted his head he took a corner of her pink-flowered curtain in his hand. 'Red hair on the pillow I like. But pink flowers on my bedroom curtains? I think not.'

Laura breathed deeply and counted to ten. 'Adam, will you please get out? I'd like to freshen up before supper.'

'You're fresh enough already,' he said.

'Do you want to eat or not?' She was *not* going to rise to the bait.

'Depends. What's for supper?' He rested his head on the window and threw her a look of velvet invitation.

'Burnt offerings if you don't hurry up and get out of here,' she snapped.

He shrugged, and gave her a crooked smile that struck her as peculiarly at odds with the unexpected bafflement in his eyes. 'OK. Just remember — in future don't call me a rat.'

Laura watched him doubtfully as he stalked to the end of her bed and stood looking down at her as if tempted to reinforce his warning. Then, apparently thinking better of it, he made for the door, threw her one last sinister look, and disappeared on to the landing. There was deep silence for a moment, and then Laura heard him running down the stairs.

He hadn't bothered to close the door, and for a few seconds she just lay there, staring at the place where he had been. Then, after a while, she ran a hand over her eyes and sat up. Supper. She was supposed to be thinking about supper. But she wasn't. She was thinking about Adam. She bit her lip. It hurt. But it didn't matter. And there was no point fooling herself any longer.

She loved Adam. She didn't want to, but she did. She'd fallen crazily in love with the most disturbing, unpredictable man she had ever met. A man who had breezed into her home with the predatory instincts of a Captain Hook, casually broken her engagement, and ended up changing her life. Because even if she never saw him again — unlikely in view of the odd thumping noises coming from the kitchen — her life had been unalterably changed.

Now she would never marry Rodney. Charlene would. But she could never marry Adam either, even in the unlikely event that he asked her, not as a kind of joke, but because he meant it. He was a dangerous breaker of hearts, a man who, whatever he might say about wearing out, would never want to change his way of life, even though, or perhaps *because* it involved danger and death.

She stood up, shoulders drooping, and walked across to the door. As she made to close it, Silver darted through the opening and streaked like an arrow for the bed. Laura sat down beside him and began absently to stroke the smooth gray fur.

No, Adam wasn't likely to change. And nor was she. After her mother's devastating desertion, she had always dreamed that one day she would be part of an ordinary, everyday family again. A family whose mother and father came home to their children every night. As she grew older, she had seen herself in the role of that loving, idealized parent.

The shadow of a leaf danced in the sunlight on the wall, and at the same moment Silver stretched out a leg and dug his claws into her thigh.

'Ouch,' said Laura. But the exclamation was only a reflex. It wasn't the cat who had hurt her. Oh, God, had she really been dumb enough to consider Adam Veryan and marriage in the same time-warp? Anyone would think she never read the papers.

He had been linked with a slinky golden-blonde socialite the last time, if she remembered. Before that a Hollywood actress.

Sighing, wishing she had never met

235

Adam, Laura bent down and buried her face in the cat's fur. If only she could stay up here all evening. If only she didn't have to face Adam again, didn't have to look into those midnight-in-the-bedroom eyes and watch him grin that challenging, come-hither grin, then she might, just *might* manage to get over him in time. As it was . . .

'Laura!' Adam's bellow roused her roughly from despair. 'How long does it take you to freshen up? Your cauliflower is turning into soup, and the burnt offering has already been accepted by the gods. Make yourself decent. At once. We're going out.'

Laura sat up with a start, dabbing at the dampness in her eyes, and Silver moved hastily out of her way. Adam was doing it to her again. Ordering her around as if it were his right.

She opened her mouth to tell him she wasn't going anywhere, but thought better of it almost at once. If supper was ruined, what choice did they have but to go out? She stumbled to her feet, and went to stare grimly at the clothes in her wardrobe. Wasn't love supposed to make you lose your appetite?

Another myth shattered, she thought disgustedly, tugging so hard at the nearest hanger that it broke.

'Laura?' Adam's voice hadn't lost any of its authority. 'Are you going to answer me, or do I have to come up there and fetch you?'

'Don't you dare,' she shouted back. 'Give me ten minutes and I'll join you.' And if he thought she meant to apologize for the demise of his supper, he could think again.

Ten minutes later to the second, Laura sailed down the stairs wearing a flared apple-green skirt and a white blouse.

Adam was waiting at the bottom dressed elegantly and dangerously in black. He nodded his approval. 'Very suitable. Prim without being austere, and properly calculated to dampen my libido. It hasn't worked, by the way.' He extended his arm. 'Shall we go?'

Laura gulped. Dear lord, he was gorgeous. Just the sight of him was melting her knees. 'On second thoughts, I'm not hungry,' she lied.

'I am.' He took her hand and tucked it under his arm. 'In more ways than one. Which appetite would you prefer me to satisfy?'

He wouldn't . . . She glanced doubtfully at the tough, piratical face, the narrowed eyes. He might. He just might. 'I suppose we'd better eat,' she said at last, trying to look as if the whole idea bored her.

Adam's smile told her he wasn't deceived for a moment, but immediately he led her outside, held open the door of his car and deposited her firmly on the seat.

The restaurant he chose this time was bright and noisy, and filled with bright, noisy young people. The only similarity between it and the Sanctuary was in the quality of the food. Laura wondered if he had picked it specifically because intimate conversation was impossible.

If so, she was grateful. She would have more than enough of intimacy with Adam in the perilous week that lay ahead. Even the thought made her shiver — and then grow uncomfortably hot when she saw him watching her with hooded, speculative eyes.

They didn't talk much on the drive back to Cinnamon Bay. Adam's face was unusually set, and she suspected that he too was contemplating the night that lay ahead. The night that she would not be spending in his bed.

Pal welcomed them enthusiastically, and in the flurry of greetings it was several minutes before Laura could turn her attention back to Adam. He was perched on a corner of the kitchen table with his hands on his thighs, lazily swinging a leg and watching her with an expression she couldn't read and didn't trust. 'It's late,' she said, glancing quickly at her watch. 'Time for bed.'

'Just what I was thinking,' he replied impassively.

Laura gulped and turned toward the

stairs. But she had only taken a few steps when she felt a peremptory hand on her shoulder. 'Aren't you forgetting something?' Adam said.

'No.' Laura's reply was emphatic. 'I'll clean up the burnt offering in the morning.'

'I wasn't talking about the burnt offering.'

She knew better than to ask what he *was* talking about, and tried to shrug off his hand. But he wouldn't let go, and she found herself being gently but firmly spun around.

'Kiss me goodnight, Laura.' His full lips parted in demand and invitation.

'No.' Laura almost squeaked. 'That wasn't part of the bargain.'

'Neither was burnt casserole,' he said softly. 'You owe me one, Laura.'

'I don't owe you anything. The burnt casserole was your own fault.'

'Maybe. But I still expect you to kiss me.'

'And if I refuse? I suppose you'll just help yourself.'

'I might. But I don't think I'll have to.' He moved one hand from her shoulder to her lower back, and pulled her in between his legs. His other hand held the back of her head. Laura could feel the hardness of his body through her thin white blouse, and as the blood in her veins began to heat she knew that if she didn't get away from him soon, her arousal would be as obvious as his was. What should she do? She forced herself to quell a rising tide of panic. Surely the quickest route to escape would be to do as he demanded? Besides, she wanted to.

With a groan of surrender she wrapped her arms around his neck, stood on tiptoe, and touched her lips briefly to his.

'Is that the best you can do?' he asked softly.

Adam's eyes were dark and deep and full of promise. He knew it wasn't the best she could do.

She groaned again, and pulled his head down until his mouth touched hers. He made no move, waiting for her to take the initiative. And with a quick, impatient movement she did, pressing her lips against his until she felt them part in response.

After that Adam swung her around, bracing himself against the wall and teasing the soft inside of her mouth with his velvet tongue. But when a familiar weakness began to wash over her in warm, sensuous waves, he dropped his arms and waited for her to pull away. After a moment, she did. He smiled, but there were deep lines across his forehead, and his mouth was forbiddingly set.

Puzzled and deeply confused, Laura stumbled up the stairs to her room and sank with a sigh on to the bed. Silver was there, twitching his tail in disapproval.

Laura lay awake for a long time that night, staring at the moon through the trees and remembering the warm taste of Adam's lips.

Why, after she had kissed him, had he

turned all glowering and introspective like that? He had been teasing when he'd demanded that kiss. Hadn't he? And why, every now and then, did she catch that baffled, frustrated glitter in his eyes, as if he felt something was happening to him that he neither liked nor understood?

She turned her head restlessly. There was no way of solving the riddle that was Adam. The sooner he was out of her life, the better.

But, oh, she would miss him so much . . .

For the next two days, Adam behaved like the gentleman Laura was quite sure he wasn't and, outside of meals, spent most of his time in the basement working on his book. Although she didn't altogether trust this suspicious lull in hostilities, she resolved to enjoy it while it lasted, and tried to keep her mind off Adam as much as possible, and on her studies.

Then on the third night everything changed.

Adam appeared for supper looking haggard, as if he hadn't slept for a week, and when Laura put his plate in front of him she saw that his mouth had twisted in a sneer.

'Now what's the matter?' she asked. 'I suppose real men don't eat shrimp salad.'

'A hell of a lot of men, and women and children, don't get to eat anything,' he growled.

Oh, so he had reached another painful chapter in his book. And, as usual, he was taking it out on her. But she wasn't willing to be his whipping girl again.

'I'm aware of that,' she said coldly, as she reached over his shoulder to retrieve the salad he had scorned. 'But as I doubt if your supper would survive the tender mercies of Canada Post, I'll just put it in Pal's dish, shall I?' She scooped the plate from under his nose and began to walk toward the corner where the dog's dish sat on a clean sheet of newspaper.

Behind her a chair scraped on the tiles, and a split-second later two arms locked around her waist and yanked her back against a muscular male body. The plate tilted dangerously, but she managed to maintain her grip.

'Put it back,' said Adam.

'Why? You don't want it.'

She felt his indrawn breath against her back. 'Trust me, I want it.'

'So does Pal.'

'I may look stupid, Laura, but I'm not. Pal has eaten his supper and gone out.' Adam's breath raised the hair on her neck, and his voice, and the feel of him, made her legs go limp with a mixture of fear and desire.

'Let me go,' she said.

'Only if you promise to behave.'

'I promise.' Pride suddenly seemed less important than escape.

Adam released her, his hands brushing her hips as he dropped his arms, and she turned without looking at him and hurried over to the table. But the moment she put down the plate, Adam spun her around and pulled her back into his arms.

'You haven't paid the penalty,' he said.

'Penalty? What penalty?'

'This.' One hand splayed over her bottom, lifting her on to his thigh. The other held the back of her neck, pressing her mouth to his while he kissed her with businesslike and excruciating thoroughness. By the time he had finished, her stomach was a fiery pool of desire.

When, at last, Laura regained control of her shattered senses, she saw that Adam no longer looked worn and haggard. He looked predatory, powerful — and yet, in some strange way, triumphant. As if he had wrestled with a personal demon and come to a decision he didn't mean to change.

She backed away from him. 'Don't worry,' he said. 'I'm not going to bite you. Yet. Fetch your salad and sit down.'

Laura, still reeling from his kiss, fetched her salad. She even made an effort to eat. But she couldn't taste her fresh shrimp.

Adam didn't attempt to talk, and Laura couldn't have found words if she'd tried.

She went upstairs soon after supper, intending to study, but she was so shaken by Adam's behaviour, and so mentally exhausted that when she lay down on the bed to rest for just five minutes she fell asleep almost at once. By the time she woke up, Saturday morning was half gone.

Adam was in the living-room reading the local paper when Laura poked her head round the door to ask if he had eaten. He said he had, and gave her a reflective look that she had a feeling was a prelude to trouble.

It was.

Half an hour later, she told him she was going into town to do her shopping.

'I'll drive you,' he said, in the sort of voice that brooked no argument.

'No, you won't.' She spoke more

sharply than she'd intended. 'I enjoy the walk.'

Adam raised his eyebrows. 'But not my company?' he suggested.

'Not at the moment.' No way was she going to tell him that she found his company stimulating, intoxicating and more than a little dangerous, but at the same time intolerably painful. She loved Adam. He excited her, frightened her sometimes, and made her feel wildly, breathtakingly alive. But the knowledge that soon he would be leaving her made every moment spent with him a bittersweet, agonizing torture that she could only endure in small doses. And after last night she trusted him less than ever. Herself she trusted not at all.

Adam shrugged and went back to his paper, leaving Laura puzzled by his easy capitulation. Usually, when he spoke in that crisp, no-nonsense voice, it meant that he intended to have his way.

Ten minutes later, when she discovered the Belvedere driving slowly beside her as she strolled along the edge of the road, she knew that today was no exception.

'Give you a lift, ma'am?' drawled Adam, tipping an imaginary cap.

'I don't take lifts from strangers driving rattletraps,' snapped Laura, getting at him the only way she knew how — through his beloved Belvedere.

Her efforts backfired. In two seconds he had pulled to a stop just in front of her, opened the passenger door, and, when she came abreast of him, reached out to drag her down beside him. Then her seatbelt was snapped into place and Adam was driving down the road at a speed that would have earned him a ticket if the traffic squad had been on its toes.

'I said I wanted a *walk*,' said Laura through gritted teeth. 'Not a highjacking.'

'I'll give you more than a highjacking if you don't watch it,' replied Adam, who seemed to be in an exceptionally ruthless frame of mind.

'What's the matter?' she jeered.

'Can't take it when a woman turns you down? It was bound to happen sooner or later.'

'I can take it,' he said. 'I'm just not taking it from you. Got that?'

The only thing Laura got was that Adam was in a very strange humour and that it would be better not to aggravate him unless she had to. So she nodded, and stared glassily out of the window.

They arrived in town a few minutes later, and the moment Adam drew up at the curb in front of the supermarket Laura opened the door and got out. She half expected him to insist on coming with her. But he didn't, and when she glanced outside she saw that the Belvedere was no longer in sight.

Probably gone to stoke up his temper at the Arms, she thought gloomily, wondering if it would be safe to go home.

Distracted, she bought more groceries than she'd meant to, and staggered out of the store with a heavy shopping bag hanging from each arm. She walked a few steps down the street, then stopped to reorganize her load. But as she bent to pick up the first bag she felt a hand brush lightly over her rear, and then the bag was swept away out of sight.

'Adam, for heaven's sake . . . ' she began angrily.

But it wasn't Adam who stood behind her leering through flabby, lopsided lips.

The small eyes appraising her neat, perspiring figure belonged exclusively to Larry Lovejoy.

8

'Give me back that bag,' said Laura furiously. 'At once. And stop looking at me like that, Larry Lovejoy.'

'Like what?' Larry grinned and held the plastic bag behind his back. 'Come and get it,' he suggested with a smirk.

'I will not. It's my bag, and if you don't give it back this minute I'll — I'll call the police.'

'You wouldn't do that to an old schoolmate, would you?' Larry went on grinning. Laura thought it was the ugliest grin she had ever encountered in her life.

'Oh, yes, I would,' she assured him.

'That's not very friendly of you.' His eyes narrowed and he took a step toward her.

Laura immediately stepped backward, and found herself pressed against the window of Mrs Alcott's dress shop. Larry continued his advance, and in a moment there was less than an inch between his long, bony body and her own. Very deliberately, he put the bag down on the pavement. Laura swallowed as she saw him lick his lips. Turning her head, she looked around for escape. There were people about, but no one was paying them any attention. She supposed that, at a glance, she and Larry looked like two lovers engrossed in intimate conversation. She could scream, of course. But she'd rather punch Larry on the nose. The days when she had been too shy and too naïve to cope with men like Larry were long gone.

'If you don't get out of my way this minute,' she began, 'I'll — '

He didn't give her a chance to finish the sentence. Her mouth was still open when he covered it with his hand and said in a flat, nasal rasp, 'You won't do anything, pretty Laura. I've been waiting a long time for you.'

Laura tried to bite his hand, but he was pressing too hard on her mouth, and her head was up against the window of the shop. She didn't believe this. Surely even Larry wasn't stupid enough to think he could assault her in the middle of the day on a busy street, with half of Cinnamon Bay doing their shopping. Then she remembered that Larry was better known for his insatiable sexual appetites than for his brains, and knew she would have to do something fast.

She started to raise her knee. But before it could connect with its target, quite suddenly Larry wasn't there. She blinked, then her eyes widened.

Larry was tall, but not as tall as the avenging angel standing behind him, gripping the neck of his T-shirt in one large, tight-knuckled fist.

'What — the — hell — do you think you are doing with my girl?' demanded Adam, enunciating each word with a slow, menacing clarity. His eyes were two furious black coals and his lips were stretched across his teeth in a feral snarl.

Laura saw Larry's pink face turn a pasty white. 'Didn't — didn't know she was anybody's girl,' he mumbled, screwing his head round in an attempt to get a look at his assailant. 'Just heard she broke up with Rodney Fosdyke.'

'Well you know now, don't you?' said Adam, shaking Larry by the neck as if he'd like to break it.

'Y-yes,' agreed Larry, who was no more famous for courage than for brains. 'S-sorry.'

Adam, apparently deciding his spineless adversary was unworthy of further attention, gave him another shake for good measure and let him go. 'And in future, keep your dirty paws to yourself,' he shouted after a swiftly retreating Larry.

Laura gazed up at Adam, who was still breathing fire, and wondered how long it would take him to cool down.

'Thank you,' she said cautiously. 'I could have managed.' When he didn't answer, but stood glaring down at her as if he thought she was responsible for Larry's unwelcome advances, she added with a spurt of irritation, 'It was kind of you but — Adam, I am *not* your girl.'

Fleetingly, she wished it weren't true, that she were indeed Adam's woman. But there was no sense dreaming of the impossible — especially now, when he looked ready to do murder.

'No kidding,' he snapped. 'And what gave that creep the idea that you're available? I thought you said he was harmless.'

'I guess I was wrong. And *I* certainly didn't tell him I'm available. Because I'm not,' Laura snapped back.

'Is that so?' Adam, his jaw jutting out like an axehead, picked up her two bags in one hand, and grabbed her wrist with the other. 'Come on, we're going home.'

As Laura had planned to go home anyway, she couldn't find the energy to protest.

The Belvedere, as she had guessed, was parked outside the Cinnamon Arms. Not that Adam could have had time to consume more than one drink before he'd come charging to her rescue like — no, not a knight in shining armour, she decided, after one wary glance at his face. He looked more like the dragon than St George.

Laura climbed into the car without demur because Adam still looked as though he was out for blood, and she didn't intend it to be hers.

'What made you come back?' she asked quietly. 'You couldn't have seen what Larry was up to from the Arms.'

'I didn't. I came back to fetch you.'

'Oh. Why?'

'Because,' he said, holding the wheel in what looked like a death grip, 'I decided a drink wasn't what I wanted.'

Laura knew better than to ask what he did want. Besides, she had a feeling she'd have her answer soon enough.

She was right. The moment they pulled into the driveway, Adam was out of the car and yanking open her door. 'OK,' he said. 'Out.'

'Did you imagine I planned to spend the day here?' she asked sweetly. She knew it wasn't wise to goad an already angry bull, but she had been ordered about by Adam once too often, and she was in no mood to take any more.

'Out,' he repeated, ignoring her sarcasm.

Slowly, taking her time about it, Laura climbed out the car. Adam seized her groceries from the back, and followed closely as she walked to the door. It was almost as if he expected her to make a bolt down the road.

Feeling his body vibrating with anger behind her, the thought did cross Laura's mind. But this was *her* home, and no bad-tempered dragon was going to force her out of it, today or any other day.

Pal came running into the hallway to greet them and provide a distraction, but unfortunately the distraction was short-lived. Adam, with confrontation in mind, was not a man to be diverted from his path. Pal sensed this and beat a discreet retreat back to his bed in the kitchen.

Adam, still scowling, dumped Laura's bags on the kitchen table. 'You can put them away later,' he said, and without waiting for her answer he put a hand in the small of her back and urged her into the living-room.

Silver and Silky were curled up on the love-seat, so Adam made straight for the sofa and sat her down.

'Now,' he said, standing above her with his hands on his hips. 'What in hell was that all about?'

'What in hell do you think it was about?' asked Laura, who was tired of being treated like a delinquent, instead of as Larry's unwilling victim.

'Don't swear,' said Adam, with astounding and arrogant irrationality. He glared down at her. 'OK, Laura Allan, it's time to put a stop to the nonsense.'

'I couldn't agree more,' said Laura.

She was glad to note that he no longer sounded like a man about to commit violence on the first thing that moved, but his mouth was still formidably hard.

'Good.' He slapped his hand against his thigh, then was silent for so long that Laura began to wonder if she was witnessing the calm before a particularly devastating storm. She watched him let out his breath, as if he'd made a decision. 'We'll be married at the beginning of September,' he said, as if he were telling her she was condemned to walk the plank. 'And, believe me, there will be no more Larry Lovejoys in your life.'

Laura was glad she wasn't holding a drink or she would have spilled it. As it was, she merely choked.

When she had recovered her ability to breathe, she lifted her head, still sputtering, and gazed disbelievingly at the hard line of Adam's jaw. 'No,' she managed to gasp. 'I mean, no there won't be any Larrys, but — Adam, you don't have to marry me just because Larry — '

'I know I don't have to.'

'Then why — ?'

'Laura, don't argue with me. This isn't a frivolous decision. I admit I've resisted the idea — '

'Adam.' Laura sat up straight and placed both hands on her knees. 'Adam, are you proposing to me? Because if you are, you're going about it in a very odd way — '

'You want me to get down on my knees? I'm not going to. But I'll start again if you like. Laura Allan, will you do me the honour of becoming my wife?' He spoke as if the words were an effort, but he managed a twisted kind of smile.

'Why?' asked Laura.

'We've been over that already. There are a number of reasons. And although I'm not anxious to give up my job, in a few years I won't have any choice. In the meantime, I'm not putting up with your being mauled about by — '

Laura moistened her lips. Her throat felt dry, and she wasn't sure if she wanted to laugh or cry. The man she loved was asking her to marry him purely for reasons of future convenience and because he hadn't liked seeing a woman he had selected for himself pounced on by the likes of Larry Lovejoy.

'Larry's my business, Adam,' she interrupted him. 'Not yours. And I don't like him any better than you do. But that doesn't mean you can put a brand on me saying, 'Property of Adam Veryan. Hands Off'. I'm not your property, and — '

'Laura.' Adam spoke with rigid control. 'You may not be aware of it, but I already have a lot more *property* than I need. What I don't have is a wife. And I don't want to brand you, I want to marry you. At the beginning of September. And if I have to put you over my shoulder and carry you to the altar, I'll damn well do it.'

Laura closed her eyes, overcome by

the erotic and unwanted images his words inspired. And she didn't doubt him for a moment. He was a buccaneer by habit and by nature, and he wouldn't think twice about carrying her up the aisle. He might have picked her out in the first place because of her unavailability — Adam liked a challenge — but it seemed that once he had his mind set on a course of action, as far as he was concerned the deed was done.

She sighed. How could she convince him it wouldn't work, when she wished so very much that it would? Was it possible . . . ?

'Laura,' Adam's voice cut through her reverie like a switch blade, 'will you give me your promise? Now?'

Laura came back to earth. Of course it wasn't possible. 'I gave my promise to Rodney,' she said wearily. 'And I broke it. What makes you think I wouldn't break any promise I might make to you?'

'I wouldn't let you.' He spoke with such easy assurance that Laura almost found herself believing.

'All the same, I can't — '

He bent down and placed a finger on her lips. 'Don't say it.'

Outside a blackbird started to sing, and two crows answered him in a ribald chorus of derision. From the basement, Howard began a persistent demand for more food. Laura stared into Adam's eyes, felt the fire of his touch bring her body to vibrant life as it always did, and tried, unsuccessfully, to speak.

At once he sat down beside her and moved his hand to her hip. Her blood leaped. She fixed her gaze on the point where his shirt opened to display the bronzed smoothness of his skin. Again she attempted to speak.

'I said don't say it,' Adam repeated, not harshly but with an air of authority.

Laura didn't say it. Instead, drowning in the dark promise of his eyes, she ran an exploratory thumb along the curve of his lower lip.

'Marry me,' said Adam, catching her wrist.

Laura groaned, as overpowering desire mingled with her love for this obdurate man until she couldn't tell one from the other. Perhaps, after all, there was no difference.

'Yes,' she murmured, because she couldn't, in the end, say anything else. 'Yes, all right. I'll marry you.'

It wasn't until she saw the way all his muscles seemed to tighten and then relax that she fully comprehended what she'd done.

From the very first time Adam had touched her she'd been lost, unable to withstand his devil's charm. And because of her own terrible weakness where he was concerned, she had agreed to marry a man who didn't love her, who thought he had a right to bulldoze his way into her life and take it over so that he would have a convenient wife to come home to when the years eventually forced him to lead a less precarious existence. And as that wasn't likely to happen for some time, she could look forward to months of loneliness, years of anxiety, interspersed with occasional whirlwind visits from a husband she might never see again. Would she be able to bear it? Should she even try?

Laura considered telling him she had made a mistake. But she hadn't really. She loved him, and if only it could work, she wanted nothing more than to be his wife. So why did she feel so desperately unhappy?

'I'm sorry, blue-eyes,' she heard Adam say, with a gentleness that for him was unusual. He was wiping tears she hadn't known were there off her cheek.

'Sorry?' Laura raised her eyes. Had she missed something?

'Mmm. Sorry I was such a boor about Larry Lovejoy.' He paused, and she guessed apologies didn't come easily to Adam. 'I know he wasn't your fault. But when I saw those great flabby hams on you, I — '

'Decided to take it out on me,' finished Laura drily.

Adam's mouth twisted. 'More or less. You see, Larry wasn't worth hitting, and you were handy.'

'That *does* augur well for our marriage,' scoffed Laura, wondering why she suddenly felt happier.

Adam put a hand over his eyes and bent his head. Laura watched him, puzzled. Did he regret his proposal, then, or merely his inexcusable behaviour? Not that it was like Adam to have regrets.

'What's the matter?' she asked, laying a hand on his shoulder.

At once he straightened and tangled her fingers with his own. 'Blue-eyes,' he said brusquely. 'Will you believe me if I tell you that whatever may happen in the future, I'll never mean to hurt you?'

Laura hadn't the heart to repeat the old cliché about the road to hell being paved with good intentions. 'Of course I believe you,' she replied.

'Good,' said Adam. 'Then it's time for us to get down to business.'

Before she knew what he was up to,

he had taken her by the elbows and shifted her back against the cushions.

'Wh-what? Wait,' cried Laura. She began to push at his hands. 'Is that why — was all this just — just an excuse to break your promise? The one you made to my father?'

She ought to have known, she thought miserably. Promises meant nothing to Adam.

He had her trapped against the arm of the sofa so she couldn't move, but as she gazed at him, angry and disappointed, she saw the warmth in his eyes fade into blankness.

'Is that what you think?' he asked, in a voice that was as expressionless as his eyes. 'How flattering.' When Laura said nothing, he added, 'Although I could have sworn you wanted me to break it.'

Yes, she had in a way. In her weaker moments. But not here in her father's house with two glassy-eyed cats looking on. She had always vowed to wait until marriage for that dimly sensed release she had never known. And even now, when she had given her word to Adam, she still wanted to wait.

His gaze held hers, cool and unloving. 'Yes,' she whispered, vaguely conscious of Howard in the basement discussing lettuce. 'Yes, you're right. I have wanted you to break it. But for me, that would be wrong. So unless you make me — '

She wasn't prepared for the pungent oath that escaped from Adam's lips, nor for the speed with which he sprang to his feet. But when he spoke, she knew she'd better listen.

'Laura,' he said, in a cold, precise tone she'd never heard him use before. 'Laura, what kind of man do you think I am? I have never forced a woman in my life, and I don't expect to start with my bride-to-be.' He rammed his fingers into the belt of his jeans and gave her a look that made her hold her breath. 'What have I done to make you think I'm a monster?'

'I — nothing.' Laura gazed up at him bravely. He looked as fierce as any of her fairy-tale villains, and yet she had a feeling that his ferocity was a front for something deeper — something that just might be pain. There was an odd, wounded look about him . . .

No, she was imagining things. Adam had no time for wounds of the heart.

But he had asked her a question, and she owed him an honest answer. 'I don't think you're a monster,' she said quietly. 'But promises don't seem to mean much in your scheme of things. Cinnamon Bay does have newspapers.'

'What's that supposed to mean?' Adam strode to the mantel, and with his back to her, picked up a long matchstick and raked it along the red brick.

'That your — your reputation isn't unknown in this town.'

Adam turned slowly, staring at the flame he had lighted until it almost burned his fingers. Then he tossed it into the empty fireplace. 'Reputation?' The word cracked like ice in hot water.

Laura realized she was still half lying

on the sofa, and sat up hastily. 'Yes. You must know that your — um — exploits, are a household word.'

'Exploits? I know that people read what I write. That, Laura, my sweet, is what being a correspondent is all about.'

'Yes, I know,' said Laura, hating the derision in his voice. 'But people also read what you *didn't* write. About your — um — '

'Ah.' Adam gazed pointedly at the ceiling. 'I begin to see. You're talking about the highly inaccurate reporting of my love-life.'

'Is it inaccurate?' She didn't want to ask, but she *had* to know.

'Not entirely, I suppose.' Unbelievably, he sounded almost bored.

'Then — '

'It is not, however, true that the world's hotspots are littered with my bastards. Or that I routinely sleep with other people's wives.'

'I didn't mean — '

'Yes, you did. Not that it matters.'

Now he sounded distant as well as bored.

'It does matter.' Laura was desperate to make him understand. 'Don't you see that if I'm going to marry you I have to know — ?'

'You don't have to know anything, blue-eyes.' He struck another match and watched it burn.

'I do. If you've left a trail of broken hearts in your wake . . . '

Adam frowned. 'I try to avoid broken hearts. I don't get off on hurting people, Laura.'

No, thought Laura. You probably don't. But that's not to say you won't do it if a sufficiently enticing prospect comes along. And as for promises . . .

'You'll hurt both me and my father if you break your promise to him,' she said quietly.

'If I . . . ' He picked up a brass elephant from the mantel, and weighed it in his hand. For a second Laura thought he meant to hurl it at her head. Then he put it down with overplayed caution, crossed the room in two strides and, taking her hands, pulled her on to her feet. 'You don't trust me, do you?' he said, sounding weary as well as angry.

'I — I don't know. I want to.' Laura felt his thumbs pressing against her palms. 'But you said — that it was time we got down to business, and I thought — '

'You thought I meant to ravish you on the spot.' Adam shook his head. 'It's a charming idea, sweet Laura, and one that holds particular attraction at the moment. But I have this old-fashioned idea that promises made to the father of my bride ought to be honoured.' He slid his hands up to her elbows and pulled her against him with an air of impatient possession. 'The business I had in mind was a kiss to seal our betrothal, and possibly a stimulating foretaste of pleasures to come *after* our wedding.'

'Oh.' Laura, who could feel the beat of his heart close to her own, unaccountably forgot that she shouldn't trust him, and lifted her lips in expectation.

Adam gazed down at her for a moment, his brow furrowed, and his eyes still curiously blank. Then he kissed her with a firm but gentle expertise that left her blood crying out for more.

'You *will* learn to trust me,' he told her when he was finished. 'Don't even think of doubting that.'

Strangely, in spite of the hard little smile on his lips and the unyielding way he held his shoulders, at this moment Laura didn't doubt it.

Then Howard's 'Ode to Lettuce' rose to a crescendo that couldn't be ignored, and Adam muttered something uncomplimentary and went to feed him.

The rest of the week passed as if the soft summer days were suspended outside of time. Adam was unusually silent, but he behaved toward her with perfect civility, keeping out of her way when she wanted to study or cook, but there if she needed help lifting, or reaching high places.

Once, a woman phoned for Adam, but when Laura allowed her suspicions to show, Adam gave a short laugh and said she was his sister. Laura didn't know whether to believe him or not. She had agreed to marry him in a moment of madness, and now realized she hardly even knew him.

At the bakery, Charlene twice accused her of forgetting to collect payment for buns sold, and in the evenings she wandered round the house in a daze, sometimes talking to Pal, who thumped his tail sympathetically, and frequently staring out of the window at nothing. On one occasion, Adam asked her whether she was watching the weeds grow or making sure the sky hadn't fallen. She didn't answer him, because what she was actually doing was wondering if this whole insane week was just a dream. It didn't seem possible that she, quiet Laura Allan from Cinnamon Bay, had got herself engaged to Adam, a man who had a girl in every airport. A man she loved, who didn't even pretend to love her back.

Sometimes, when he was being particularly polite and reserved, she wondered if Adam even liked her. Then she thought that perhaps his unusual reluctance to do battle was merely his way of earning her trust? On the other hand, maybe he just wanted to drive her crazy.

If so, he was doing a masterly job.

On Saturday, when Laura arrived home from work, she discovered Adam hadn't been idle while she was out.

'The second weekend in September,' he announced across the supper table as he helped himself to another serving of pasta.

'What?' Laura raised her head and gave him a puzzled frown.

'I said the second weekend in September. I've booked the church, organized a few friends, and my sister Ann is bringing the kids, the Cadillac and a new man.'

'Oh.' Laura swallowed. 'Don't I have any say in the matter?'

He shook his head. 'In the matter of the date? No, my sweet, you don't. As to flowers and guest-lists and all those other frills that go with weddings, you're on your own. Until the honeymoon, when you most definitely will not be on your own.'

Laura swallowed again. 'Honeymoon?'

'Mmm. Paris, of course. And I thought perhaps Venice. Maybe Vienna as well.'

Just like that. Paris, Venice, Vienna . . .

'Something wrong?' drawled Adam, taking a slice of garlic bread.

Laura shook her head. No, there was nothing wrong. Except that . . .

'Adam,' she said, getting up and standing with her back to him at the sink, 'are you sure you really want us to get married? Because if you don't — '

'I'm sure.' His voice was brusque to the point of rudeness, and she heard his chair scrape back. But before she could move, his arms had closed around her ribcage.

'Laura,' he growled into her ear, 'do you honestly think that after thirty-five years of single bliss, I would drift into marriage by accident?'

'No,' she whispered. She could only manage a whisper because his touch made her feel dizzy, as if she'd been knocked off her feet. 'No, I guess I don't.'

'Then perhaps it won't surprise you to know that once I've made up my mind I rarely change it.'

'No. No, it doesn't surprise me.'

'Good. Because I've made up my mind to have you.' He slid his hand over her stomach. 'You won't get away.'

Laura didn't want to get away. She supposed that must be why she had agreed to marry him against every sane and sensible instinct she'd ever had. For a moment, as she felt his lips touch her hair, hope flared, burned brightly, and then faded. Adam had loved Christine. He wouldn't love again, and he wasn't marrying her for love, but for posterity — for the children who would carry on his name.

'I have things to do,' she said abruptly. If she didn't get away from him at once, she would either burst into tears or start making love to him on the spot.

'What things?'

'Just — things. Please let me go.'

Adam let her go, so quickly that she fell against the counter and hit her arm. At once his eyes narrowed. 'Laura? Are you hurt?' He spoke roughly, but his eyes were surprisingly soft. Almost as if he actually cared . . .

'I'm all right,' she said. 'Adam . . .'

'Yes?' He bent down to pat Pal who had just come padding into the kitchen.

'Adam, there's something I have to ask you. You say you find me attractive — '

'Mildly.' He straightened, arching his eyebrows at her and giving her a small glimpse of his teeth.

Laura was in no mood to be teased. 'Please,' she said. 'I'm serious. I need to know if — I mean — oh, dear.' She groped for a tissue and found the dishrag. 'What I'm trying to say is, do you think there's a chance that someday you may come to . . . ?' She stopped, unable to get the words out. She *couldn't* ask him outright if he thought he might someday learn to love her. Because if he said no, the future would be too bleak to contemplate.

Adam waited for her to finish, and when she didn't, with one smoothly efficient motion he hauled her back into his arms and put a finger under her chin to tip up her face.

Laura held her breath, hoping, and yet afraid to hope.

'If you're asking me what I think you are,' he said, 'then the answer, for what it's worth to you, is — ' He broke off as Pal started to bark.

Seconds later a door was flung open in the hallway, footsteps sounded, and a familiar tuneless voice began to bellow, ' 'Fight the good fight with all thy might.' Laura! Adam? I'm home.'

9

Adam muttered something she didn't catch, and Laura released her breath and said reluctantly, 'I think you'd better let me go.'

'Why?' He tiled his head back to get a better look at her. 'Did you know you've turned a most unbecoming puce?'

She probably had, but more from frustration than embarrassment. Adam had been about to answer the question she hadn't been able to bring herself to ask. If he had not been interrupted, by now he might have spoken the words she had waited so anxiously to hear. Or, of course, he might not . . .

Laura bent her head and fixed her eyes on his feet. 'Just let me go,' she said wearily.

But Adam didn't let go. Instead he looped an arm around her waist and urged her out into the hall.

Lancelot, surrounded by suitcases, was serenading a wriggling, ecstatic Pal.

'You're home early, Dad,' said Laura, trying hard not to sound resentful.

'Humph. Suppose I am.' Lancelot turned, his nose slightly redder than usual, blew a gust of air through his moustache and swallowed visibly.

Laura, distracted by the seductive pressure of Adam's fingers on her back, didn't take in that her father was behaving like a bashful schoolboy, and asked brightly, 'Was Mr Leversage pleased to get his book back?'

'Hmm?' Lancelot looked startled. 'Nope. Couldn't give it to him. Poor fellow got himself run over by a moose.'

'What?' Laura forgot about Adam's fingers, which were working their way down her hips, and gave all her attention to her father. 'Did you say he got run over by a *moose*?'

'That's it. Keen hunter, old Leversage. Moose turned the tables on him.'

Laura hastily banished a vision of old

Leversage's head adorning the walls of some complacent moose's lair, and tried to make sympathetic noises.

In the end it was Adam who brought the subject back to Lancelot and his early return by asking what he'd done with Mrs de Vere.

'Primrose? Freshening up at her place, she says. Be over when she's finished.' He cleared his throat and added gruffly, 'Asked her to marry me. Said she would.'

'Dad! That's wonderful.' Laura pulled herself away from Adam and ran to fling her arms around her father. 'Oh, I am so happy for you. And now I won't have to worry about you and Ethan, when — if — when Adam and I . . . ' She paused, and Lancelot glanced up sharply.

'No ifs about it.' Adam spoke crisply from behind her. He placed a proprietorial hand on her shoulder. 'Laura and I have news for you as well,' he said to Lancelot.

'Hah. Thought so.' Lancelot nodded,

looking pleased with himself. 'Going to marry my girl, are you? That's the ticket. Knew it would all work out.'

'Dad!' exclaimed Laura. 'So you *did* leave me with Adam on purpose. I'm not a pawn in some chess game, you know.'

Lancelot didn't answer, but only because, with his customary talent for evasion, he was already halfway up the stairs.

Adam chucked her under the chin and said, 'The queen, my sweet. Never a pawn.' Then with an irritating grin he swung Lancelot's baggage over his shoulder and followed his host up the stairs.

The queen indeed, thought Laura, glaring at his muscular back. Not that it makes much difference. Pawn or queen, either way I've been played for a patsy by my own father.

She stamped back into the kitchen to clean up, not sure whether she wanted to laugh, cry or give both her father and Adam a hearty kick in the pants. On general principle the latter would be the most satisfactory, she decided, but the probability of retaliation was too great.

Laura sighed. Then the sigh quivered into a reluctant giggle, and she began to pile dishes in the sink.

She was only half finished when she heard a boisterous female voice from the hall telling Lancelot he was supposed to be saluting his bride. This was followed by loud laughter and the sound of very audible kissing.

Laura smiled and turned on the tap.

Half an hour later she found herself perched on the edge of a chair in the living-room, biting her lips and trying desperately not to laugh as her father and Primrose gave an involved and deadly serious account of the events leading up to their engagement. These, apparently, had included a liquid celebration in Robson Square with old Keating, old Symes and old Bronowski which had caused a busload of African tourists to make an unscheduled stop to study the mating rites of *homo Canadianus*.

'Damn cheek,' muttered Lancelot.

Laura could see the laughter dancing in Adam's eyes, and wasn't surprised when he excused himself suddenly and vanished through the door with unseemly haste.

She murmured her own excuses and followed him out.

At once, and without even troubling to look round, Adam extended his arm backward and drew her to him.

'What do you think?' he asked, his voice shaking suspiciously. 'Shall we contribute our bit to culture and have an engagement celebration of our own?'

Laura stopped wanting to laugh.

'No,' she said abruptly. 'There isn't anything to celebrate.' Safe in the circle of his arm, she had glanced up in time to see a familiar look of mockery in his eyes, and it brought home to her how much more secure and happy Primrose was with her father than she could ever hope to be with her enigmatic, unpredictable Adam. And she felt tired, confused, frustrated, and reasonably sure she'd been insane to agree to this marriage.

She waited for Adam to respond, hoping, in spite of herself, for reassurance, for some indication that he cared, even a little.

But his mouth had hardened, and he only pointed her in the direction of the stairs, said, 'Don't be contrary, blue-eyes, it doesn't suit you and I don't like it,' and gave her a smart pat on the rear. When she turned to glare at him, he added, 'Goodnight, sweet dreams, and make sure you sleep off that bad temper.'

'What if I don't?' snapped Laura, who was in a very bad temper that seemed to have overtaken her out of nowhere. Obviously it had to be Adam's fault.

'If you don't, you'll upset your father. Also I don't mean to put up with it. Now go to bed. And don't you dare get up on the wrong side.'

Dictatorial jerk, thought Laura, searching her brain for a sizzling retort. When one didn't come to her, she was forced to remember that she hadn't much use for temperament herself. Perhaps Adam had *some* reason to criticize. But not to dictate. And *his* temper wasn't always the sweetest.

'*Goodnight*,' she said shortly, turning her back on him and heading up the stairs to her room.

It was a warm night, but Laura found she didn't mind the extra warmth of the two cats who insisted on sleeping on top of her. They provided just the kind of soft comfort she needed on this night when her whole world seemed about to fall off its axis. Her father was engaged to Primrose de Vere, and in a few weeks she would be married to Adam. It was a strange thought.

What kind of marriage could they hope for, she and Adam? *He* might be content with the satisfaction of his bodily needs and a brace of children. But she needed more than that. She wanted to be much more than Adam's lover and the mother of his children. She wanted to comfort him when he hurt, make him laugh when he was sad, be there for him when he needed her — and for him to be there for her.

But he had never promised her that. So how could he be sure he would honour his wedding vows? After all, he didn't pretend to love her.

Laura fell asleep vowing that in the morning she would confront Adam, and ask him the question to his face. That way she would know for sure whether she was a fool in love, or just a fool to hope. She twisted restlessly on the bed. There *had* been that moment, before her father came home, when for a few seconds she had seen something in his eyes . . .

Yes. In the morning. She put an arm around Silky and went to sleep.

But in the morning she awoke much later than usual and, as it was Sunday, she didn't get up right away. Then the phone rang and she pushed back the covers. But somebody answered it, so she fell back on the pillows, unwilling just yet to face the day.

When she did finally make her way downstairs she found Lancelot in the kitchen reading the paper. Two egg-stained plates supplied evidence that Adam had cooked breakfast for them both. Pal, snoring on the floor at Lancelot's feet, had a faint yellow moustache around his lips.

'Where's Adam?' asked Laura, trying to sound casual as she took out a bowl and began to fill it with cereal.

'Hmm?' Lancelot looked up. 'Phone call. Some woman. Think it was your friend from the bakery. Said something about her needing his help. Anyway he went out.' He returned to his paper, obviously seeing nothing odd in Charlene's requesting help from his daughter's fiancé when she had a perfectly good fiancé of her own. Well, Rodney, anyway.

Laura finished her breakfast in a thoughtful mood, and after she had washed up, she pulled on a pair of shorts and a T-shirt, and told her father she was going for a walk. Then she made her way down the road to the turn-off that led to Charlene's lodgings in the basement of an older, woodframe house painted white with bright green shutters.

There was no answer when Laura knocked at the back door, so she tried the handle. It turned easily. Inside, a wooden plank had been laid across wet linolcum in a passageway leading to the door of Charlene's living-room. Thinking she could hear voices, Laura picked her way toward the sound.

When she reached the door she stopped dead.

Adam's low, sexy baritone was murmuring soft, indistinguishable words to someone she couldn't yet see.

A slow-burning pain twisted deep in Laura's gut, and when she threw the door wide it wasn't the dim lighting that blurred her vision, but a blinding swell of unshed tears.

'Laura!' Adam's surprised and unrepentant voice hit her like a cold glass of water. 'What are you doing here?'

Laura didn't answer. She couldn't, because in the light cast by the small basement window she could see that he was sitting on Charlene's sensible brown sofa with his arm draped around her friend's waist. Charlene was leaning up against him, her head drooped on to his shoulder and her dark hair just tickling his chin.

'Laura?' Adam repeated, with a hint of censure.

'I . . . ' She tried to find something to say. Anything that wouldn't betray her overwhelming sense of desolation and sense of betrayal. But all she could manage was, 'I don't know. I shouldn't have come,' before she turned to dash blindly from the room.

She reached the door without knowing quite how she got there, and was groping for the handle when she tripped on the end of the plank. As she clutched at the air for support, her hand closed around a solid human arm.

'Laura, what the devil do you think you're doing?' Adam demanded as he yanked her upright. 'What's the matter with you?'

'Nothing,' she said, in a high voice she didn't recognize as her own. 'Why should anything be the matter?'

Adam opened the door and pushed her up the steps and into the sunlight. 'I've no idea, but you're behaving like a hysterical — '

'Schoolgirl,' finished Laura in the same unnatural voice. 'How original of you, Adam. But isn't that exactly what you signed up for? Someone young and unsophisticated who would bear your children and not notice when you had a torrid little fling with some dark-haired siren — '

'*Charlene?* Are you calling Charlene a dark-haired siren? Now listen, you idiotic redhead . . . ' He thrust his face into hers and his eyes were as black and angry as she had ever seen them. 'It's time you stopped reading fairy-tales.

I'm no Prince Charming, God knows, but neither am I the Big Bad Wolf who seduces the innocent virgin. Charlene is engaged to the worthy Fosdyke — '

'So was I, but that didn't stop you seducing me.' Laura tried to pull away, but his big hand only tightened on her elbow, and she could almost smell the scent of his anger.

'In case you haven't noticed,' he rapped out, 'I have not — yet — seduced you. That, my sweet, is a pleasure yet to come.'

'It's not going to come,' shouted Laura, who was now so desperately confused, and crazed with grief, that she scarcely knew what she was saying. 'I *saw* you with your arm around Charlene. How can I possibly marry a man I can't trust not to make love to my friends?'

'Make love to . . . ?' Adam's nostrils flared, and he used a word Laura hadn't heard before. 'Laura, I was not making love to your friend. I was dealing with a flood, if you must know — '

'Sure. That's exactly what it looked like,' she jeered.

Adam's eyes turned as bright and hard as black diamonds, and this time when she made to pull away, he didn't attempt to prevent her. Expecting resistance that didn't come, she tumbled over on to the grass.

He made no move to help her up, but stood looking down at her with his hands on his hips and his lips curled in an improbable sneer. 'OK,' he said. 'Have it your way. I'm a callous breaker of hearts who can't be trusted. So why don't I dig myself in deeper and prove it beyond any doubt?'

Laura could hear the beating of her own heart. She gazed up at him in anguish, unable to believe what she was hearing. Then with a quick impatient movement he bent down and hauled her to her feet.

She stared at him, stunned and disoriented. Then suddenly she was enfolded so tightly in his arms that there wasn't any question of breathing. She opened her mouth to cry out. At once he covered it with his, kissing her with such rough, savage passion that the world around her was no longer grass and sky and trees, but a scorching red heat that threatened to reduce her, not to ashes, but to a melting pool of unsatisfied desire.

When, finally, it was over, she discovered that her feet had left the ground. Adam was holding her suspended against his thigh in one sinuous arm.

He lowered her slowly, letting her T-shirt ride up her body, and when she looked down, still dazed, she saw two ladybirds settle on his forearm.

He waved them off, and she watched their flight into the blue, wishing she could fly away with them, away from all human pain and doubt. But Charlene was standing in the doorway looking worried. She was wearing a white robe stained with dark spots and a big white towel was draped across her arm.

'Laura,' she began, 'I hope you don't think — '

'She does,' said Adam, over his shoulder. 'But I've given her something else to think about. Haven't I, Laura? Come on, Charlene, let's get on with finishing what we started.'

Without looking at Laura again, he took Charlene by the arm and drew her back into the house.

Laura watched the door close, heard the sharp click of the lock, and felt the bright morning sun touch her back. But it couldn't warm the deep chill that had settled over her heart like a blanket of ice in midwinter. The bitter taste of loss was in her mouth.

She turned slowly, and like an automaton, began the endless walk home. Each step seemed like a lifetime of shattered hopes. Hopes that, until Adam, she hadn't even realized she had. They were gone now. Adam might try to tell her there was nothing between him and Charlene, but her eyes hadn't deceived her, and she knew exactly what they'd seen — Charlene and Adam close together on a sofa, engaged in a blatantly amorous conversation. And afterwards Adam had gone back into the house with Charlene to — what had he said? To finish what they had started.

Oh, he was dealing with a flood all right, Laura thought bitterly. A flood of passion. And, unbelievably, he seemed to expect her not to mind. It was as if he imagined their wedding could still go ahead.

And yet, when he had kissed her just now, she had thought for a few shining seconds . . . No. She must forget about that. That kiss had only been Adam's way of demonstrating the power he wielded over her senses. As if that power had ever been in doubt!

When Laura arrived home, the first thing her dreary gaze lit on was the Belvedere, a poignant reminder of intoxicating hours spent with Adam. She knew then that she couldn't bear to go into the house. Her father would start singing Adam's praises. And then he would start talking about weddings. Hers, as well as his own.

She hesitated only briefly before dodging past the windows and into the woods behind the house.

Her secret place was green and soft and quiet, as it always was, but this time its peace failed to soothe her. She kept thinking of the last time she had been here. Adam had come . . .

As she sat on the moss listening to the laughter of the stream, Laura wondered if this woodland sanctuary would ever work its magic on her again. After a while, she wrapped her arms around her legs, dropped her head on to her knees and waited for the catharsis of tears.

But her pain was too deep, and the tears wouldn't come.

It was afternoon by the time she returned to the house, belatedly re-membering lunch. She hoped Adam hadn't come back. She didn't think she could face him just now. In fact if he refused to leave Cinnamon Bay at once, she would go herself. Primrose could look after her father, so she wouldn't be leaving him in the lurch.

Laura needn't have worried. Only Lancelot sat in the living-room, smoking his pipe and looking dour. 'Adam's left,' he told her at once. 'Said you wouldn't want him around.'

'Oh.' Laura didn't feel up to answering the accusation in her father's eyes. She was too stunned.

She had wanted Adam to go, of course she had, but — would she never ever see him again? Never was so final. So —

'How — when — will he be back?' she finally managed to croak.

'Didn't say when. Or if. Said you wouldn't care.' Her father beetled his eyebrows disapprovingly. 'You're a fool, girl. Good man, Adam.'

Yes, she was a fool all right, Laura silently agreed. But not because Adam was a good man. Adam was an unprincipled, self-centred rogue who had spent a lifetime doing as he pleased. How could she have thought for one moment that he might change?

'I'll go and get lunch,' she murmured dully to Lancelot. As she left the room, she felt his eyes glaring at her back.

They ate lunch quickly and without much conversation, and as soon as they were finished Lancelot went to visit Primrose. Laura cleared the table and started the washing-up. Then she went up to her bedroom to study. An hour later, she realized she had read the same paragraph on Messalina for the seventh time. And always she pictured the wanton empress as a dark-haired seductress with her head resting on the shoulder of an emperor who bore a disturbing resemblance to Adam.

Halfway through the afternoon Laura gave up, and went down to the basement to see for herself that Adam really had gone.

He had. The room where he had lived for so many weeks contained only furniture and Howard. The guinea pig sat mumbling in a corner of his cage as if he too were conscious of his friend's departure from his life.

But Howard would forget Adam the moment someone else gave him lettuce. It would take more than lettuce to make Laura forget.

The doorbell rang, and she frowned and went upstairs, expecting to do battle with a salesman.

But it wasn't a salesman who stood on the step fidgeting with long silver earrings.

It was Charlene.

Hail Messalina! thought Laura viciously. But she said nothing, and only stared at her erstwhile friend, determined to hang on to her pride. There wasn't much else to hang on to.

'Can I come in?' asked Charlene, when Laura didn't move from the doorway.

Silently Laura stepped back. She didn't want to talk to Charlene, or have anything further to do with her, but she was damned if she would wear her heart on her sleeve. With Pal trotting at her heels, she led the other woman into the living-room, which reeked of Lancelot's pipe, and waited for her to sit down.

Charlene chose the least comfortable seat in the room, an upright wooden chair with a hard back, and crossed her legs self-consciously. Laura slumped down on the loveseat.

'Laura,' Charlene began, twisting a button on her blouse. 'Laura, I came because — because you're my friend, and I think you've got the wrong idea. About me and Adam.'

'Oh?' Laura raised her eyebrows. 'And what idea would that be?'

Charlene blinked. 'You sound like the Queen of Hearts in *Alice in Wonderland*. Are you about to say 'Off with her head'?'

'No.' Laura spoke quietly. 'I wouldn't go that far.'

'But you *are* mad at me. Aren't you?'

'I'm trying not to be.' It was true.

There wasn't much point in staying mad at a person you had to work with. Especially when the real cause of your anger had already walked out of your life.

'Then please don't be,' said Charlene, leaning forward and clasping her hands on her knees. 'And don't be mad at Adam either. He was only doing me a favour.'

'Oh, yes? And what sort of favour was that?'

'Laura, *please* listen. And do stop being the Queen. It really wasn't what you think.'

Laura thought of asking, 'And what *do* I think?' But she decided against it. It would be easier all round to let Charlene get whatever she had on her conscience off it. As quickly as possible. Then she would leave. 'All right,' she said. 'What is it you want me to hear?'

Charlene uncrossed her legs. 'I had some trouble with my drains,' she explained. 'Adam was quite amazingly helpful.'

This time it was Laura's turn to blink. 'Drains?' she said faintly. 'Adam was amazing about *drains*?' She saw Pal's ears prick up and knew he hoped they were discussing food.

'Well, yes. You see, some roots had grown into the plumbing and everything backed up through my kitchen. There was water all over. The Atagis upstairs were out, and — well, I guess I got a bit panicked. So I phoned you. And Adam answered.'

'Why didn't you phone Rodney?' asked Laura, holding a hand to her head. She felt faint. As if the room were revolving around her.

'He's in Vancouver for a few days on business. Besides . . . ' Her voice trailed off.

Besides, thought Laura, Rodney wouldn't have been the slightest use about plumbing. She discovered she was holding her breath as she waited for Charlene to go on.

'So anyway, Adam came right over. And you needn't have worried, because

I promise you I wasn't a pretty sight. I'd started a nosebleed, and there was blood all over my face and on my robe. Adam was wonderful. He called a plumber and mopped up the blood, and helped me clear up the mess, and — and . . . '

'And stayed to collect his reward,' said Laura bitterly.

'No. No, it wasn't like that. The flood had destroyed my new carpet, and I guess I was more upset than I realized. I started to cry, and — and Adam made me sit down, and he put his arm round me and made me wipe my eyes, and then you came in and — oh, Laura, I didn't mean to cause trouble for you and Adam — '

'You didn't,' said Laura, at last releasing her breath. She still felt as if her heart had been flattened into a pancake, but she was beginning to suspect, too late, that she might have misjudged Charlene royally. With a sigh, she muttered, 'Adam doesn't need any help to be trouble.'

'But it wasn't his fault.' Charlene's protest was sincere. 'He didn't do anything he shouldn't have. After you left, he came in and helped me finish the cleaning up, and then he said he had to leave town. I thought — I thought he was leaving because you'd told him to.' Her dark eyes widened with regret.

'Adam does as he pleases,' said Laura. 'Not as he's told. And I didn't tell him to go.'

Charlene frowned. 'I don't understand. Why *did* he leave, then?'

'Because he was angry, I suppose.' Laura watched Pal's tail twitch in his sleep, and wished that she too could escape into dreams. But for her the dream had ended when she woke up in Charlene's basement suite, and jumped unerringly to the wrong conclusion. Of course Adam was angry. No wonder he'd left.

'He told me I had to learn to trust him,' she told her friend, with a break in her voice. 'But I couldn't. I didn't believe him when he said he was only helping you deal with a flood. I thought — well, everyone knows he has a reputation that rivals Casanova's — '

'Undeserved, I think.' Charlene smiled. 'No paternity or breach-of-promise suits.'

Laura tried to smile and failed. She drew her bare feet up on to the loveseat. 'Maybe you're right. But it makes no difference. Because when it comes right down to it, he doesn't love me, and — '

'Laura, are you out of your mind?' Charlene's voice rose along with Pal's ears. 'Adam's crazy about you.'

'What makes you think that?' Laura brushed a hand across her eyes. 'If he loved me even a little, he wouldn't have left.'

'He would if he thought it was hopeless. Does he know you love him?' Charlene leaned so far forward that she almost fell out of her chair.

'Is it that obvious?'

'To me it is. Oh, Laura, I am so sorry — '

'No. No, don't be.' Laura laid a restraining hand on her friend's arm. 'I'm the one who has to apologize. For thinking you would — would — '

'Steal your man when I'm lucky enough to have Rodney,' Charlene suggested with a grin.

That hadn't been precisely what Laura had in mind, but it was close enough. She nodded weakly. 'Yes. That's it.'

'Don't worry about it,' said Charlene. 'Just go and get your Adam back.'

'Yes,' agreed Laura doubtfully. 'Maybe I'll try.'

But she had a feeling that an angry Adam who had made up his mind that she was too insecure and too lacking in trust to suit him, might not be easy to get back. Because he *didn't* love her. Charlene was wrong about that. And if she tried to rekindle the flame, to prolong the agony, might she not end up even more lonely and desolate than she was now? Time, after all, was supposed to heal even the bloodiest of wounds.

Laura heaved another sigh, and Pal ambled over and pushed his nose under her arm. She rubbed his ear abstractedly. It was true enough that Adam didn't love her. But it was also true that a small kernel of hope was once more beginning to flower in her heart. Charlene had been so sure, so definite . . .

Yes, she would try to find Adam. And when she did, she would forget her pride, and let him know that she loved him. Beyond that . . . beyond that she wasn't willing to think.

But by the time another week had passed she had given up thinking at all, and the kernel of hope had shrunk to the size of a dust speck.

Adam appeared to have vanished from the face of the earth. It was as if he'd taken up covering wars on another planet.

Laura's first move had been to track down his sister in Vancouver.

Ann said that, yes, Adam had stormed into the house, snarled at the dog, frightened the kids, packed a kitbag and stormed out again looking as if he meant to start his own personal war. When Laura asked if he had said where he was going, Ann replied that he'd *said* he was off to shake the daylights out of, and some sense into, a certain redhead — but she didn't think he'd really meant it.

'No,' Laura had agreed gloomily. 'He didn't. I'm the redhead. And he's not shaking any daylights out of me.'

She almost wished he was though. Anything would be better than the awful, dead emptiness she felt every time she heard Howard chirp, or her father start to hum the 'Wedding March'. It seemed that wherever she went in the house there was something to remind her of Adam. His absence was an almost tangible presence, and that didn't make a whole lot of sense.

But then nothing made any sense. Although she scanned the papers for news of Adam's whereabouts, she found not a word either by him or about him, and when she checked with the major news services no one had any inkling of where he might be.

She began to wonder if the only place he existed was in her heart.

September came, and Ethan returned from Victoria. When school started, he took Howard and all the other denizens back to class, and after that the house seemed even emptier than before. Laura remembered how Adam had admired Demetrius's reproductive prowess, and felt her throat close up at the thought that now she would never bear his children. And it was her own fault. Adam had been right all along. If she had trusted him, in two weeks they would have been married. And miracles sometimes happened. It was possible he would have learned to love her.

But not now. Now she didn't even have that hope.

Then one evening when she came home from the bakery, Lancelot announced that he and Primrose were getting married on the second Saturday in September.

'But that's . . . ' Laura bit her tongue. That was the day Adam had set for their wedding. Had her father forgotten? Or was he completely unaware that his daughter might find that date painful?

'Problem?' grunted Lancelot, knocking his pipe on the edge of the kitchen table. 'Don't see why.'

'No. No problem,' whispered Laura as she ran from the room.

She didn't see her father's concerned gaze on her back, nor did she heard him mutter, 'Damn fool girl. Ah, well, won't be long now,' before he returned his attention to his pipe.

Upstairs in her room, Laura flung herself down on the bed, scattering two indignant cats, and gave way to the tears she'd been holding back for weeks.

A long time afterwards, it occurred to her that at least now she was able to cry. Maybe that was the beginning of healing.

Two weeks later, wearing an ivory silk dress with a high neck, fitted bodice, and a skirt that fell from her hips in soft folds, Laura stood with Primrose de Vere and Primrose's brother, Anson, at the entrance to St Matthias' Church. Primrose had insisted that Laura was to be her only bridesmaid. She had also insisted on the dress.

'But I can't wear ivory,' Laura had objected. 'That's for brides.'

'Not when the bride is past sixty,' said Primrose firmly. 'This bride is wearing sensible bottle-green. And if I want my bridesmaid to wear ivory on my special day, surely you can indulge an old woman.'

Match point to Primrose, thought Laura, who didn't really care what she wore. Ivory it is.

And ivory it was. As Laura stood in the bright sunlight trying not to think of how different this day might have been, Primrose took her gently by the arm and turning to Anson said, 'Come along, my dears. The church is full, the

314

groom is waiting and the organist is playing 'There's a Friend for Little Children'. We'll find ourselves being christened if we don't hurry. Harry does get a little confused.'

For the first time since she'd got up that morning, Laura caught herself smiling. This was her father's and Primrose's day. She wanted it to be happy for them, even if she couldn't be completely happy herself.

The three of them mounted the steps and were greeted by Ethan and another smiling usher whom Laura was surprised to find she had never met. Then they waited for Harry, the organist, to switch gears. It took a little time to convince him he wasn't playing for a christening, but finally the strains, not of the ponderous 'Bridal March' but of Grieg's 'Wedding Day at Troldhaugen' floated down the aisle.

Trust Harry, thought Laura, waiting for the music to change.

But it didn't, and Primrose's fingers tightened on her elbow. 'Forward,' said her father's determined bride, as if she were sending troops over the top. 'Time to get the show on the road.'

Laura moved through the high, arched entrance and on into the chancel of the church. And as the joyful passion of the music surrounded her, and the sun cast blue beams through stained glass, she thought for a moment that she was dreaming. Her father was waiting as expected. But the man beside him, in the position where the groom was supposed to stand, looked just like Adam.

Laura closed her eyes and continued a swifter than usual progress down the aisle. She didn't open them again until she heard Anson cough discreetly behind her. She would have fallen then if firm fingers hadn't grasped her by the arm.

'Hello, blue-eyes,' whispered Adam, his dark eyes deep with warmth and affection. 'I've missed you. Have you, by any chance, missed me?'

10

Laura swayed forward and found herself leaning against Adam's body for support. But when she heard a faint, amused murmur coming from the congregation behind her, she remembered where she was and stood up straight.

'Adam,' she whispered back, fighting to gain control of her whirling senses. 'What — how . . . ?'

'It's the second Saturday in September. I told you we were getting married today.' His smile was firm, as sexy as ever, but . . . no. This couldn't be happening.

Laura glanced over her shoulder. Was she going crazy? *She* wasn't getting married. Primrose was. To her father. But Primrose was standing behind her, smiling smugly. On the other side of Adam, Lancelot stood with his hands behind his back looking like a general who had just pulled off a particularly tricky battlefield manoeuvre.

'Yes, this is *your* wedding-day, dear,' whispered Primrose. 'Your father and I were married very quietly last week. It was what we wanted.'

Laura stared at the blue sunbeams on the wall. She heard the soft murmur of the congregation, smelled the sweet scent of gardenias and felt Adam's touch on her arm. In the midst of confusion, he seemed the only solid reality. She turned to look up at him and saw that, although he was still smiling as if he hadn't a doubt in the world, there was strain, and uncertainty behind the warmth in his eyes.

Their gazes locked. Laura's mouth was dry, her face hot. She wanted to ask a million questions, to tell him that this whole scene was insane, a plot cooked up by a madman with the aid of her lunatic relations. She still wasn't sure she wasn't either crazy or dreaming. Then all she knew was that, crazy or not, she was happy.

Adam said, so quietly that only she could hear, 'Laura, I want you for my wife. Now and for always. But the decision has to be yours. If you say no, I won't trouble you again.'

That was when she knew this was no dream, but the turning point of her life.

She opened her mouth to reply, but no words came. After all the weeks she had spent searching for Adam, could he really be here, waiting in the church for her on exactly the day he had planned, with no word to her, but obviously with the collusion of her family. She wanted to ask him why. But it wasn't the time. Behind her a congregation of her friends was waiting to see her married to the man she loved. The man whom, for a few seconds, she had an astonishing desire to kick sharply in the shins. But it wasn't the time for that either.

Adam had asked her if she'd missed him. She had. Desperately. Hopelessly. And if she said no to him now, she would miss him for the rest of her life. Questions and recriminations could wait.

Smiling with a hard-fought serenity, she lifted her chin and said clearly, 'Yes.'

'Thank God,' whispered Adam, and Laura thought she heard him release his breath.

A faint stirring of relief rustled through the assembled friends and family as Lancelot moved to Laura's side, and the stranger who had ushered them in stepped forward to stand beside Adam. Then, and with only a very slight raising of the clerical eyebrows, the Reverend Archibald Oliphant stepped forward to perform the age-old rite that would pronounce Adam Veryan and Laura Allan husband and wife.

★ ★ ★

'Why, Adam? Why?' Laura stood facing Adam across the big bed in the suite booked for the first night of their honeymoon. The venerable, Elizabethan-style hotel on the outskirts of Victoria had an atmosphere of old-world charm and unostentatious comfort. But Laura was in no mood to notice anything but the crimson-quilted bed and, peripherally, a paved pathway outside the window which led down a steep incline to the sea. Not much of an escape route, she thought, a little wildly. And Primrose had packed so many suitcases for her, she'd be obliged to leave most of them behind.

Adam loosened his tie, removed his jacket and slung it over a chair. 'Why what? Don't you like the room? We can always change it.'

Laura ran her tongue over lips that felt unusually dry. Soon, inevitably, he would take off more than the jacket . . . She watched as he unfastened his cuffs and rolled up the sleeves of his shirt. 'This isn't a game,' she said, swallowing. 'You know I'm not talking about the room. I want to know why you disappeared like that. And why you and my family planned *my* wedding without telling me about it.'

'I did tell you. Several weeks ago. And you agreed.'

'That's just it. You *told* me. Didn't it occur to any of you that I might like to have a say in the matter? Was it necessary to *trick* me into marriage?'

'I didn't trick you. I said the decision was yours.' He made it sound as though there was nothing unusual about being asked to make that decision in front of a church full of people who were waiting for the reverend to marry another couple. At least, that was what she had thought at the time.

'Sure you did,' she agreed. 'And you also said that if I turned you down you wouldn't trouble me again.'

Adam pushed a hand through his hair. It fell across his forehead, shading his eyes and making him look more untamed and unpredictable than ever. 'That's right. I didn't want you to think I'd continue to disturb your life if you didn't want me. Besides . . . ' He smiled wryly. 'The only kind of trouble I can give you is exactly the kind I hope you want. But you had to find that out for yourself.'

Laura clenched her fists tightly against the silk of the ivory dress she hadn't bothered to change, and prayed that she would be able to maintain control long enough to get Adam to talk sense. She had managed to smile and nod her way through the wedding, and the reception at the Sanctuary afterwards, only because it wasn't in her nature to make a public exhibition of herself. It had helped too that most of the guests had been aware of the deception and thought it romantic and amusing. Adam's best man, an old friend and fellow reporter, and Adam's sister, Ann, had come from Vancouver especially for the occasion. If Laura had indulged her inclinations, and told Adam exactly what she thought of his machinations, she would have been judged an ungrateful and unromantic harridan, and he would have come out looking like a blameless and misunderstood white knight. Which he surely wasn't.

In the car on the way down to Victoria, she had refused to speak, and Adam had made no attempt to break her silence. But once or twice he had thrown her an oblique glance — and smiled.

He never knew how close that smile came to landing them both upside down in the ditch.

But now they had reached their destination, and it was time for the game playing to end. Time to lay her cards on the table.

'Yes,' she told him. 'You're right. It seems you are the one trouble I can't stay away from. I knew it as soon as you left town. That's why I've been trying to find you ever since.'

Adam nodded. 'Yes, I know you called Ann. She told me.'

'I called everyone. Nobody knew where you were.'

'A few people did. Not Ann. She'd have told you.'

Laura turned away, too hurt and confused to face him any more. 'Why was it necessary to humiliate me?' she asked, in a voice she fought hard to keep steady. 'You must have known — '

'All I knew,' he interrupted, 'was that you had so little faith in me that you believed I would seduce your good friend. Laura, ever since the day I first met you you've looked on me as some kind of chauvinistic stud, out to break the heart of every passably attractive woman I set eyes on. And you hated yourself for succumbing to my dubious charms — '

'But I was engaged to Rodney.' Laura's wail of protest sounded unconvincing even to herself.

'Whom you didn't love. Don't give me that, Laura. Rodney was just a smokescreen you hid behind because you couldn't let yourself trust a man with a reputation for changing partners. You didn't bother to find out if that reputation was wholly deserved — '

'It wasn't just your reputation,' Laura interrupted. 'You deserted Christine because you wouldn't be tied down, you had no compunction about detaching me from Rodney, and your job — well, your job doesn't go with settling down.'

'I know. So I left you on Charlene's back lawn. In a flaming rage, I admit. Later, after taking a hard look at the feelings I hadn't been willing to come to terms with, I realized I had to give you time — '

'Time for what?' asked Laura, gazing without focus at the wall.

'Time to find out what you wanted,' Adam answered. 'Oh, I knew you wanted me in your bed.' He gave a short, bitter laugh that for no good reason made her heart beat faster than it should. 'But you weren't at all sure what you wanted in the long term. Were you? If I'd come back any sooner, you'd have got cold feet again, and been so damned busy looking for reasons to doubt me that eventually I'd have been driven to some form of satisfactorily neanderthal reprisal. Which would have given you the perfect excuse to call off our wedding. Better, even, than finding me consoling Charlene. I felt you needed to be alone for a while to work out for yourself what you wanted.'

'Yes, I see. It worked. I missed you.' Laura stared down at the cream-coloured carpet and scuffed its pile with her nylon-clad toe. 'But you could have told me you hadn't cancelled the wedding. There wasn't any need for the deception?'

Out of the corner of her eye, she saw a movement, and thought Adam meant to come to her round the bed. But he stopped still the moment she looked up.

'If I'd told you, you might have gone into reverse and dredged up a million other reasons not to trust me. And I'd had about all I could take. As it was, you were forced to confront the fact that, as far as you knew, I'd gone for good. And to my eternal relief, I think you discovered you didn't like it.' He flashed her a smile so brief it was more like lightning forking through a cloud.

'You still could have told me,' said Laura.

'Yes. I suppose I could. But I chose not to give you the chance to talk yourself out of going through with it. Your father, who knows you a lot better than I do, said I was more than likely right to do things my way. He and Primrose have been a great help.'

'Oh,' Laura was momentarily bereft of words. In a way, she could understand Adam's reasons for acting as he had. She hadn't given him much reason to believe she wouldn't change her mind. But surely her family must have known . . .

No. On second thoughts, how could they? Her father only pretended to be vague. The truth was, he never missed a thing. Of course he'd observed her antagonism to Adam — and argued with her about it.

'I didn't mean to humiliate you, blue-eyes,' said Adam softly, as she gazed past him and refused to meet his eyes. 'I *did* mean to marry you, though, and I was fairly sure that, faced with a *fait accompli*, you would do — '

'Exactly as you wanted me to do,' said Laura bitterly.

'Yes. Which you did. Are you sorry?'

Laura looked at him then. There was something in the way he'd spoken that, for one of the few times since she had met him, made her think he was actually capable of self-doubt. And he had gone to extraordinary lengths to make sure she didn't turn him down. Could that mean . . . ? Was it possible . . . ?

He was frowning, watching her with that stern, guarded look she had always found it impossible to interpret.

'No, I'm not sorry,' she said at last, her lips parting in the first smile she had given him since they left the reception. 'I might have gone to the church kicking and screaming if I'd known it was

329

my own wedding. But I'd have been there.'

Adam's shoulders seemed to relax and, very briefly, she saw him close his eyes. Then he laughed softly and reached up to pull off his tie. 'In that case I apologize. I misjudged you. And I too was guilty of lack of trust. But as the prospect of carrying my bride kicking and screaming to the church didn't appeal to me — '

'Really? I'd have thought it was exactly your style.' Laura batted her eyelashes at him.

'Hmm?' Adam looked startled. His eyes narrowed. 'On second thoughts, maybe it is.'

To her astonishment, he leaned across the bed to grab her hands. Then he was dragging her over the crimson quilt. As she turned on her side to gape up at him, he said calmly, 'No, I'm not altogether sorry I arranged things the way I did. And now, if you don't mind, I'd like us to get on with the honeymoon.' He sat down on the bed and reached for the fastening of her dress.

'What if I do mind?' murmured Laura into the covers.

'Try kicking and screaming and you'll find out,' replied Adam amiably.

'But we haven't unpacked yet.'

'Quit stalling, Laura.' He pulled the dress down off her shoulders and rolled her on to her back. Then he looked down into her eyes, and his own expression softened. 'Don't you trust me even now?' he murmured, smoothing the long hair back from her forehead. 'Don't you know I'd never hurt you, beautiful blue-eyes?'

And Laura did know. As all her doubts and reservations fell away, she linked her arms trustingly around his neck and waited for the honeymoon to start.

Soon the ivory dress lay on the floor, along with Adam's shirt and trousers, and as his lips moved to the hollow of her neck, and then down lower, Laura curled her fingers in his thick pirate's hair and whispered, 'Adam. Aren't you forgetting something?'

He lifted his head at once, dark eyes startled and wary. 'We're married, Laura,' he said. 'I thought you wanted — '

'Oh, I do,' she assured him.

'Then what — ?'

'There's something you haven't told me.'

He propped himself up on one elbow, and frowned down at her. 'What are you talking about? I — '

'Something you haven't *said*,' explained Laura.

'Ah. I think I get it.' His eyes cleared, and he gave her the warmest, most sensuous smile she had ever seen. 'How could you doubt it, lovely Laura? I love you. Did you imagine for a moment that I would have gone to all this trouble if I didn't? I may not have known it until I left you — in fact I'd persuaded myself I was marrying you for every reason but the true one — but when I thought it was all over for us I found that without you my life had very little meaning.' He tugged gently at a lock of her hair. 'Of course I *should* have known you were my one and only woman the day you fell at my feet and said, 'Ouch.' Or later, when I went into orbit over Larry Lovejoy. And perhaps, in a way, I did know. I was sorely tempted to flatten Fosdyke too.'

Laura smiled back at him, knowing that all the love she bore him was shining out of her eyes. 'I'd have said more than 'ouch', if I'd known what I was in for,' she teased him. 'But I'd still have loved you.'

Adam laughed softly as his hand began a gentle exploration, stroking the smooth skin of her inner thigh. 'Shall I show you all the ways I love you?' he murmured, dropping a featherlight kiss on her nose.

'Yes, please,' said Laura, running her palm over the firm, bronzed skin of his back.

And Adam did.

★   ★   ★

'Just think,' said Laura. 'If Dad hadn't found you in the pub, and if I hadn't burned the dinner and fallen at your feet so you had to notice me, I'd still be engaged to Rodney, and — '

'Blue-eyes,' said Adam, the laughter in his eyes belying the severe line of his mouth, 'I am not an item of lost luggage your father found. There was never a chance you'd be married to Rodney. And no man in his right mind could fail to notice you. So please don't get the idea you need to burn food in order to attract my attention, because I promise you it won't be the kind of attention you're after.'

Laura laughed up at him, loving the way the wind lifted his hair, tossing it in disarray around his face, turning him into her very own wild man.

It was early morning, and they were standing by the railing on the hotel terrace watching the waves crash against the rocks. The sun was warm, the air was clear, and she felt as if she held the whole world in her arms. As in fact she did, because for the moment her whole world was Adam.

She knew that in time reality would rear its prosaic head. Life with Adam would never be predictable or easy. They would quarrel, and sometimes get angry. But in the end they would always work things out. After last night she could never doubt that. Adam had indeed shown her all the ways he loved her, gently, expertly and most beautifully. And she had returned his love with all the pent-up need and passion she had been saving, without knowing it, for this wonderful, exciting man who had won her heart.

'Adam . . . ?' she murmured now, as a seagull dipped its wings above their heads, and she was reminded of flight and faraway places.

'Mmm?' He rested his cheek on her hair. 'What?'

'We haven't talked about it, but when we get back from Venice and Paris . . . ' She paused because she still couldn't believe that tomorrow she would really be in Europe. 'When we get back, where are we going to live? Or rather, where am I going to live while you're off chasing battles around the world?' She spoke quickly so the words wouldn't stick in her throat. 'I mean, I suppose I could stay on in Cinnamon Bay. Jerry's hired someone else for my job, but — '

'Hold it right there.' Adam laid two fingers gently across her mouth. 'First of all, I have no intention of leaving my new wife while I go off chasing battles. Second, you are not staying on in Cinnamon Bay. Your father's house is Primrose's province now — '

'No, it isn't. He's moving into hers.'

'Even more to the point, then. Third, if you want to finish your degree, the quickest way to achieve that is university. And I don't suppose it's escaped your notice that Cinnamon Bay doesn't boast an institute of higher learning. Or that it does contain Larry Lovejoy. Do you really think I'd waltz off to the ends of the earth knowing Larry was just waiting to get his tentacles on you?'

'No, but you know he wouldn't get the chance. So — '

'So, my sweet, adorable, apparently feather-brained wife, you are living with me. Full-time.'

'All right,' said Laura agreeably. No way was she going to rock this totally unexpected boat. If Adam proposed to stay in one place, she would be there if it turned out to be the South Pole. Which, knowing him, it might very well be. She glanced up at him with doubt in her eyes. 'Where?'

'Toronto probably. I'm going to be working for national TV. I signed the contracts three days ago.'

Not the South Pole, was the first relieved thought that sprang to Laura's mind. But was Adam voluntarily giving up the chance to get his brains blown out on a regular basis? It didn't seem likely.

'So that's where you were,' she murmured. 'And I thought you were off trying to get killed.'

'My sweet,' he drawled with a certain malice, 'while it's true that you have frequently driven me to thoughts of murder, the idea of suicide never once crossed my mind.' He stroked his hand lightly over her hip, and the seagull, now sitting on the sea wall, let out a raucous demand for a handout.

Adam was in one of his sarcastic moods again, Laura noted with amusement. Well, two could play at that game.

'I see,' she said gravely. 'Does that mean you've taken a nice, safe desk job, and plan to grow too fat and lazy to do anything but eat? Because if it does — '

She was interrupted by the sound of Adam's low growl in her ear. 'I'll give you fat and lazy,' he threatened. 'And I'll show you I can do a lot more than eat.'

Before Laura could catch on to what he was up to, Adam had swept her up in his arms and was carrying her through a lobby filled with open-mouthed hotel guests, and up the wide staircase to their bedroom.

'I hope this isn't going to become a habit,' sighed Laura, remembering several occasions in the past when he'd played the caveman.

'Could be,' muttered Adam, dumping her on to the bed.

After that he proved that he could indeed do a lot more than eat, and Laura forgot about food altogether until Adam remarked smugly that they'd missed breakfast, and would miss their plane as well if they didn't hurry.

He didn't sound at all concerned, and Laura realized that she would have to get used to living with a man who didn't worry about missed connections any more than he worried about personal safety. Which brought her back to the matter of Toronto.

'What are you going to do for national TV?' she asked him doubtfully half an hour later, as they sat in the back of a limousine speeding down the highway to the airport. 'Write TV news?'

'Sometimes. I also plan to make it.

In-depth investigations, some on-the-spot reporting and announcing. Whatever comes up. Of course it will involve travel at times . . . '

Ah. She'd known there was a catch. And from the sounds of it Adam wouldn't be staying out of trouble for long. He had always lived in the eye of the storm. But at least now the storm wouldn't automatically involve bullets and bombs.

'Won't you mind?' she asked, resting her cheek on his shoulder as he settled her more comfortably against him. 'I mean, being in one country most of the time?'

He put a fist under her chin and lifted her face up. 'When that country contains you? How could I mind?' When she only stared at him, he added with a wry quirk of the lips, 'Yes, all right. There will be times when I'll miss my old life. But sooner or later I would have had to face a career change in any case. Now seems as good a time as any.' He bent his head and planted a kiss on

340

her lips. 'Especially when I have an impossible blue-eyed redhead to keep me busy. And now let's talk about weddings.'

'Weddings? We just had one,' exclaimed Laura. 'Not that I had much to do with it.' A faint feeling of resentment returned to mar her euphoria.

Adam nodded. 'I know. That's what I want us to talk about.'

When Laura looked up in surprise, he explained, 'I told you I did everything my way because I loved you too much to take a chance on your backing out. But that doesn't mean I felt good about it. Ann told me I was a cad and a jerk, and I have an uncomfortable feeling she's right.'

He actually sounded guilty. Laura contemplated rubbing it in and getting her own back, then thought better of it. She loved this man. He had done what he did because he loved her. There could be no satisfaction in salting the wound.

'It doesn't matter,' she said quietly,

turning to look out of the window and noting with surprise that they were almost at the airport.

'It matters to me.' He put his hands on her shoulders and pulled her round to face him. 'Laura, Ann says that every woman deserves to have the wedding she's always dreamed of. With flowers, and bridesmaids, her own choice of music — the whole bit. I deprived you of that — '

'No you didn't. I had flowers and happy music. And Primrose.'

'Who was supposed to be the bride. Blue-eyes, I know it wasn't fair of me, so as soon as we get back from our honeymoon I want you to start planning the wedding you've always wanted. Spare no expense. Drive me crazy with decisions about decorations, music, guest lists — anything you want. And this time we'll do the thing right. There's no law says we can't have two weddings. It's done all the time.'

It was a tempting offer. Especially the part about driving him crazy. But she couldn't take him up on it.

'No,' she said, shaking her head and taking his face in her hands. 'I've never been one for a lot of fuss and fittings. There's only one item I ever wanted at my wedding.'

Adam frowned. 'What was it? I can give it to you — '

This time it was Laura's turn to place her fingers on his mouth. 'You already have,' she told him, with a smile that was pure provocation.

His frown deepened, emphasizing the darkness of his eyes. 'What do you mean? What was it you wanted?'

Laura's smile was no longer teasing, but soft and gentle with love. 'You,' she said. 'You're all I wanted. And you were there. Waiting for me at the altar, with a look in your eyes I'd given up all hope of seeing. What more could I possibly ask?'

Adam made a sound that might have been a laugh, but was probably a groan, and pulled her into his arms.

The limousine drew to a smooth stop

outside the airport, and when the gray-haired driver came round to open the door he discovered his passengers lying across the seat locked in an embrace that showed no signs of breaking up for hours. He smiled, remembering his youth, and coughed discreetly. When discretion brought no response, he knocked on the roof. Still no reaction from the couple on the seat.

With a shrug and a sympathetic chuckle, the driver gave up and closed the door.

Adam and Laura missed their connection to Paris.

But it didn't matter, because they missed it together.

THE END

We do hope that you have enjoyed reading this large print book.

Did you know that all of our titles are available for purchase?

We publish a wide range of high quality large print books including:
Romances, Mysteries, Classics
General Fiction
Non Fiction and Westerns

Special interest titles available in large print are:
The Little Oxford Dictionary
Music Book, Song Book
Hymn Book, Service Book

Also available from us courtesy of Oxford University Press:
Young Readers' Dictionary
(large print edition)
Young Readers' Thesaurus
(large print edition)

For further information or a free brochure, please contact us at:
Ulverscroft Large Print Books Ltd.,
The Green, Bradgate Road, Anstey,
Leicester, LE7 7FU, England.
Tel: (00 44) **0116 236 4325**
Fax: (00 44) **0116 234 0205**

HER HEART'S DESIRE

Dorothy Taylor

When Beth Garland's great aunt Emily dies, she leaves Greg, her boyfriend, in Manchester — along with her successful advertising job — to return to live in Emily's cottage. Feeling disillusioned with Greg and his high-handed attitude, she finds herself more and more attracted to her aunt's gardener, Noah. But Noah seems to be hiding from the past, whilst Greg has his own ideas about the direction of their relationship. Surrounded by secrecy and deceit, how will Beth ever find true love?